The Watchmaker 2

B.L. Blocher

The Emerald City Press—Southington,CT
ISBN: 978-1-7374610-0-5
Library of Congress Control Number: 2021913369
Title: *The Watchmaker 2*
Author: B.L. Blocher
Digital distribution | 2021
Paperback | 2021

This is a work of fiction. The characters, names, incidents, places, and dialogue are products of the author's imagination, and are not to be construed as real.

Thewatchmaker1939@gmail.com

Dedication

I am honored to dedicate this book to my dear friend Elyahou (Eli) Parzivand. A wholesale jewelry vendor, who had migrated from Israel and settled in East Longmeadow Mass. He would often stop at my jewelry store in the early 90's and we instantly connected and became good friends.

With his heavy Israeli accent, he often spoke of his family and his time in Israel where he was an Israeli war hero, who courageously battled in many Israeli conflicts. One of which, he bravely fought to recapture Jerusalem from Arab control during the memorable 1967 Six-Day War.

I remember him brazenly stating to me that he was the 6th Israeli soldier to place his hands on the great Western Wall when they reclaimed Jerusalem. "It was ours again", and he proudly held up six fingers on his hand, to convey to me that he was at the forefront of the fighting. Whenever he would enter my shop, he always had a smile on his face and he would cheerfully refer to my mother as Ma and my father as Pa. He came by often, at least once a week, and he was always happy and would robustly laugh about some sort of funny story he thought was amusing. My mother couldn't resist Eli and fawned over him, and she treated him like a son. They both had a sort of connection. She recognised the fact that while he was fighting for Israel, he was fighting for her, a

Holocaust survivor, and for all the other survivors and jews all around the world. I suppose my mother considered them both to be survivors in their own right. Eli Parzivand, such an incredible person. A courageous man of honor, dignity, integrity and righteousness.

But most of all, a friend who was loved by everyone who knew him.

Introduction

I suppose it's human nature to armchair critic what someone should have or could have done in the unfortunate event of being held captive by merciless and evil monsters such as the Nazis. Couldn't someone have overwhelmed a guard and wrestled a gun away from them, or try to gang up on a few of those bastards? Not being in their shoes it's difficult to contrive what went on in the minds of the imprisoned and downtrodden. They all knew that they were being systematically murdered.

Why not at least take a few of those scoundrels down. Maybe they just hoped they would be spared if they didn't rock the boat, so to speak. But then there were some like my parents, who were clever, smart, they knew how to make things happen. They jumped at opportunities and they knew how to try to manipulate the system, just barely enough to squeak by. There were many others too like my parents, but luck had a lot to play in their survival. A turn here, a pause there, someone's look the other way, could make the difference between life and death. I think the reality of it was, you had to be extremely lucky to have made it out of the Holocaust alive.

The Watchmaker 2: The Chosen is pure fantasy fiction. In my mind I contrive the "what if's and the why not's" in life, and then a story begins to unfold in my mind. Whatever I write, I do so under the veil of "Writer's Privilege". What does that exactly mean? It means that it's my story and I get to play it out the way I see it. Yes, my stories, although sometimes based on true events, are but pure fantasy. That's why I invented Joseph the Watchmaker and his righteous clan of combatant children. Each one of them has their own unique personality that I can call on.

It would have been ideal if all those Nazi scoundrels never would have made it out of Germany, and they all faced their consequences "Short and Sharp". But many, and some of the most notorious ones got away, without facing any punishment.

In my mind, I found a way to fictionally seek out my own personal justice. Even if this story is obviously pure fiction with fictional characters, places and events. The three barbaric and diabolical monsters that I write about in this story were real and so were their horrific endeavors. The three of them...Muller, Heim, and Mengele, three of the most notorious Nazi's to crawl out of the cesspools of Hell, and they all seemed to escape justice. In my fantastic story, I exercise my right to "Writers Privilege". And so the story goes....

Chapter 1

Almost eleven years have passed since we arrived in America. My father and I work together at our watch and jewelry store in the heart of the jewelry district in Manhattan.

My father has just turned 55 this year and although his hair is now totally gray, he is as fit as an athlete.

His hands are strong from opening and working on difficult watches.

I am amazed at the fact that he can easily break a walnut with his bare hands, but then in contrast, while repairing an intricate watch mechanism, he can delicately set a tiny watch spring gear with the utmost precision. It's amazing to me.

Our lives continued to be difficult without my mother. There is a large black hole in our lives that haunts us each and every day. My father has done everything he can to be both a father and a mother to Hanna and me, but he lacks her softness.

I think what I miss most is my mother's gentle touch, and her comforting way that always seemed to make us feel better when we were sad or sick.

It's just not the same when my father throws a wet face cloth on my face when I have a fever, as opposed to my mother gently wiping my forehead and putting her soft cheek against mine to see if my fever has gone away.

I miss that tenderness she once shared with me. I miss her so much.

I constantly have night terrors about the Holocaust and our journey to freedom. But I do sometimes have wonderful dreams.

Dreams in which my mother and grandparents come back to me.

It feels so good when that happens. For a moment I have them back and I can be with them once again, although it's not always a happy ending.

However, those dreams are few and far between, and mostly they just end abruptly with Nazis or that bastard Wolfie killing everyone.

My father never wanted to remarry, even though there were plenty of Matchmaker busy bodies coming into the shop, and trying to "Make a Match" for him.

He never had the desire to find a new wife.

"I have all the love I need from my children.

I don't need the headache of a gold digging woman," he would say whenever he was asked why he never remarried.

But the truth of the matter was, he could never find another woman that he could love as much as our mother.

No one could ever replace her.

My father occasionally communicates with Dombrovsky by mail at least several times a year, and sends him packages of goods. Unfortunately his two daughters left him, and they ran off with a pair of Russian soldiers they had met when their town was liberated by them.

He now lives on the farm with his wife and youngest daughter, and those dead Nazis buried underneath his manure pile.

Fritz, the German pilot who flew us out of Poland, recuperated in Stockholm, and sat out the war until he was able to send for his family.

They quickly migrated to the United States, and he now owns an air freight company based in Florida called "Gold Coin Air Freight."

He sometimes comes to visit whenever he lays over in New York, and he always brings us a can of sardines and seltzer water as a joking remembrance of our rough landing in Sweden!

Hanna is in high school and will be graduating next year. It's amazing that she remembers only a very little, and has been suppressing most of those horrendous memories. But she does remember throwing up the sardines when the plane landed so roughly on the beach in Sweden. To this day though, she still hates fish!

It's been difficult for her too, growing up without our mother. Fortunately she turned out to be a very lovely young lady.

My father has been warding off the boys, scaring them away with war stories of killing and torturing the Germans.

"It would be easy to make a few teenage boys disappear if they choose to chase after my daughter!" he would brag.

Of course he was just kidding around with them, sort of.

Hanna wants to become a lawyer, and is hoping to attend Yale after she graduates high school next year.

My father thinks it's pointless and she should just work in the shop with us.

But she is determined to save the world, and he can never say no to her wants and desires.

Someday she will do something important. There must be a reason why she survived, why we all did.

I've personally met many young ladies throughout the years.

However, none was able to capture my heart. I suppose the events of my childhood made it impossible for me to settle down as Benny did. But maybe someday I'll find that special person who can tolerate my suitcase full of mental Holocaust baggage.

For now, I'm just happy working with my father every day, and I have the freedom to do "whatsoever" I want. I'm only twenty-three. I have plenty of time to settle down.

Benny and Sonya had left New York after a few years and immigrated to Israel.

They wanted to help settle the fledgling country, and

together they joined the Haganah. The small Israeli army which also accepted women to fight for their freedom.

They fought together against the Arabs, and the Germans who aided them as they raged war on Israel. The Germans unconscionably taught the Arabs the art of guerrilla warfare, and how to fight and kill the Jewish settlers. Some things never change.

The young couple were ferocious fighters in the army, and were instrumental in liberating the country and forming the new state of Israel.

They were both selected when the Mossad (Israel's elite secret police) was formed, and they are now high-ranking agents. Although Sonya took time off to start a family, she still continues to work for the Mossad.

The pair were known throughout the world to be an effective and ruthless killing machine. Especially when it came to destroying the enemies of the state, and hunting for Nazis who escaped prosecution after the war.

After all, Benny did have a personal axe to grind.

He used all the documentation that he claimed from the plane to help hunt and identify hundreds of Nazi perpetrators.

They have two little girls, one year apart Rachel, named after Sonya's mother, and Gitel, after Benny's mother.

They are five and six years old, and a handful for Benny.

We often write letters to each other and occasionally we even speak by telephone. I wish we could see them soon, I miss my brother and his family.

My father persistently asks him when he is coming back to New York, and he always replies;

"Short and Sharp, Papa. Short and Sharp!"

Our jewelry store is lucrative and very busy.

My father continues repairing watches, while I am mostly out front, helping customers and selling watches and gold jewelry.

It's interesting dealing with so many different people every day. There is a lot of kibitzing with customers and learning about their past.

Most items we sell become important family heirlooms.

Every item that comes in for a repair has a story behind it.

A great grandmother's lost ring that was found in the drain of a sink twenty years later, or a jilted brides engagement ring that turned out to be worthless. We've seen it all!

Chapter 2

One early Summer afternoon, just before closing, I noticed a middle-aged man, dressed in a white short-sleeved dress shirt, black pants and a black fedora hat.

He was carrying a brown weathered valise, and wandering outside the store. He was pacing back and forth, and would frequently stop only to peer into the large glass windows of our shop.

Then he would start for the door, then stop and check again, peering through the glass door to see if there were any customers still inside.

Clearly he was waiting for everyone to leave before he was going to enter our shop.

I became concerned that he might be a robber, or even worse, a wholesale jewelry vendor!

When the store was finally empty, the man hesitantly wandered in. The old doorbell jingled as he entered and he looked up at it.

He was a short and stocky middle aged man, with a large square face and golden gray hair.

He had sadness in his eyes, along with a stark cold frown.

As he approached me, I had a sense that I knew him, even though I had never seen or met him before.

He reminded me of the many other Jewish survivors I had encountered. Lost souls trying to understand why they survived while so many others in their families perished.

They somehow seem to have pieces missing from them, and it's something that we alone can recognize, although it may not be apparent to others.

The visitor carried his old abused briefcase in his right hand, and he stopped in front of the glass display case that separated us.

"Good afternoon, my name is Boris Wilensky," he stated. Then he raised his left hand to shake hands with me.

I noticed his hands were large and thick with very sharp pointed fingernails, and his voice was heavy with a strong European Jewish accent. Awkwardly I reached my left hand over the display case to greet him.

I instantly noticed that several numerical digits were recklessly tattooed on his inner forearm.

Immediately I recognized the significance of those numbers, and I was instantly taken aback and drew a heavy breath. He was an Auschwitz concentration camp survivor.

He was one of the chosen few that had emerged from one of the worst hell hole concentration camps the Nazis devised to exterminate Jews and other virtuous people.

They tattooed numbers on their prisoners forearms to keep track of them.

In doing so they had made them into inhuman objects, rather than people with names.

I stared deeply into this man's dark eyes, and I could see into the blackness of his soul.

He was alive, but not living. If he had survived that horrific concentration camp, most likely he was already dead inside and just carrying on as a zombie.

His thick hand engulfed my hand and he squeezed it firmly.

He knew I instantly recognized the fact that he was a survivor when he saw me react when I noticed his numbered arm.

"My name is Jacob. Let me get my Papa. I think he would like to meet you, too." I said.

I hurried back to the workshop to get my father.

"Papa, there is an Auschwitz survivor in the store!" I shockingly whispered.

"Does he want to buy something?" my father asked.

"I don't think he is here to buy, but maybe to sell. He has a briefcase," I replied.

When I returned with my father, the man was still standing in the same place and staring into the mirror mounted on the wall behind the display case.

He seemed to be looking right through the mirror, as if it were a window.

He was seeing or searching for something we ourselves were blind too.

My father extended his right hand and introduced himself.

"Welcome, landsman, I am Joseph," greeted my father.

"I know who you both are," replied the man.

Again it was his left hand that he offered to my father.

And, he continued to tightly grasp his briefcase with his right hand.

My father awkwardly changed hands to accommodate the man.

"My name is Boris Wilensky. I learned about your heroism during the war. You killed many of those bastards that were murdering us. And, you and your boys gave those Nazi demons the deaths they deserved. Not to be executed in a humane fashion, as the world courts would have it. But to give them what they deserved for their cruel and merciless atrocities. You sent them back to the fires of hell where they came from. Justice was served by you and your children," he paused.

"Where is the Shecket's boy?" he continued.

"Benny is in Israel," my father replied.

Boris looked disappointed.

But then he noticed the gold watch on my wrist, and he asked if he could see it.

I pulled up my sleeve revealing my beautiful watch that my grandfather had made for me.

Boris stood there and gazed at it with appreciation.

"My, that watch caused a lot of trouble, but I'm glad you got it back from that Nazi bastard," he said.

Meanwhile my father was becoming anxious and curious why Boris had come to see us.

"What brings you here my friend?" questioned my father.

The man put his briefcase down on the glass showcase and began telling us his horrific story.

"As you can see by my serial number imprinted on my arm, I am a survivor of Auschwitz. One horrific night the Nazis raided my home in Krakow, Poland. We had been hiding up in our attic behind a false wall for some time, until the Germans were tipped off by my Polish neighbor, and their blood thirsty dogs led them right to us. They brutally took my wife and me along with my two identical twin boys. They were little... just six years old," he paused to take a heavy breath.

My father and I stood solemnly and listened.

"We were severely beaten and loaded like animals into cattle cars onto a train with hundreds of other Jewish families.

My wife and I embraced each other, and placed the boys between us to shield them from the other people that were pushing and shoving against us. We were packed so tightly we could hardly move. We clung to each other as we heard children crying, women screaming and men praying. We were trapped in there for three days with no water, food or a place to go to the bathroom. The smell was sickening and we took turns to breathe the fresh air coming in from the barred window.

We all prayed that when the train stopped, the doors would open and there would be a grand paradise awaiting us.

Instead we were introduced to an inferno worse than hell.

As we were forced off the train, we saw a sign made of iron positioned over the main entrance gate saying 'Auschwitz...Work Will Set You Free' so I thought at least we had a chance to get out of there if we worked hard.

The Nazis made us immediately strip off our clothing and then put us into a long single line in the middle of the compound. A shriveled stone-faced demonic son of a bitch wearing tiny wire glasses sat comfortably at a little table at the end of the line. He was the one who had the power to point us where to go. Either to the left or to the right. One way meant immediate death. The other meant you likely would live, maybe a few more days or more if you were lucky.

The sadistic devil showed no emotion or hesitation. It didn't matter if you were a child or an adult. He just stared coldly at you and efficiently wagged his boney finger, and decided our fate.

My boys and I were directed to the right and our forearms were tattooed immediately with no compassion or indifference. My wife was sent to the left and I never saw her again. We didn't even have a chance to say goodbye. She was herded into the showers, but instead of water, poison gas filled the room and most everyone was killed. If you were still alive when the chamber doors opened, you were either shot or bludgeoned to death," he sadly paused again.

"My sons and I were sent to a barracks where there were other child twins and children who had either blond hair, blue eyes or something unusual about them. Most were alone, afraid, and crying and hoping for their parents to find them. I don't know why I was allowed to accompany my boys, other than they had a use for me at the camp.

The following morning we were awakened, as guards entered our barracks. They were escorting a short black-haired officer, dressed in an official black SS uniform. He had monstrous low eyebrows and a space between his two front teeth, and he wore a white lab coat over his uniform which was stained with splatters of blood. The guards referred to him as "Doktor".

We were forced to march through the mud into a concrete block building which contained a monstrous surgical laboratory. We were oddly lined up and we stood against a wall of beautiful scenic pictures of South America. As the doctor walked through the group, he grabbed at the children's hair and tugged at their body parts, scanning their attributes and looking into their mouths. When he came across my two twin boys, he ordered his henchmen to immediately take them away!

I grabbed my sons and pulled them in close to me! Engulfing my arms around them! I embraced them tightly with all my might! I refused to let them go! I locked my arms around my sons and clenched my hand around my wrist so tightly that I still have the scars from my fingernails. I heard the doctor shout at me,

'Let them go! Don't worry Juda, you can have them back when I'm done with them!' and he maniacally laughed.

The guards began hitting me with sticks, but I still would not let go of my children! Suddenly I was knocked in the back of my head with something hard. They tore my boys away from me as that Nazi doctor continued to laugh. That beast was Dr. Josef Mengele," Boris somberly stated.

"Mengele!!" my father horrifically exclaimed.

At Auschwitz he was known as "The Angel of Death!"

He chose prisoners to be his human guinea pigs for heinous experiments, and he was especially intrigued by twins, trying to unlock the secrets of genetics, and to discover a way to create the ultimate Aryan race.

He was the scourge of the earth.

Even to say his name was difficult and gut wrenching.

He was truly evil as he tortured and killed thousands of men, women and children with his barbaric experiments.

"I was hit again!" Boris continued.

"My head was split open and I was knocked unconscious. They dragged me out, and dumped me onto a pile of dead naked bodies. A prisoner, who noticed me moving, dragged me off of the pile and into his barracks. I was barely alive, but he slipped a sugar cube into my mouth and the sweet taste made me feel at peace.

Being unconscious felt so good, I was floating and I dreamt that I was in a beautiful paradise! Until I was harshly awakened, then my dream changed from paradise to a horrible nightmare. When I opened my eyes, I realized I was lying on a filthy wooden floor next to a pail of urine and feces. Many strange sunken faces were gazing down at me, and wondering who I was and if I was going to survive.

"Why did you bring me back from my state of euphoria?!

I felt I was free!" I moaned to the man who had saved me. I then realized my savior was an old friend from my town. "Boris, don't let these monsters take away your dignity and life!" he shouted at me.

My head was pounding, but I realized I could not help my boys if I was dead! The men in the barracks hid me for a few days as the back of my head healed. I learned that the men in this barrack were forced to carry the dead bodies from the gas chambers to the cremation ovens. At one time they were living breathing humans who were loved and gave love, and now they were turned into the walking dead themselves, lost souls and empty shells of who they once were.

Sadly, sometimes they even had to unconscionably carry their own family members or friends from the gas chambers to the cremation ovens. But they trudged on, burying their emotions deeply. They had no other choice. They had to do whatever they had to do to survive. But, no one could last very long mentally, doing this horrific chore. They usually lost their minds after a few weeks and jumped onto the electric fence which surrounded the camp, or they just let themselves be executed by the Germans," Boris paused.

My father and I stood silently as we dredged down our emotions and tried to contain our tears.

"Each day I desperately tried to get to my sons, but the area was heavily guarded. Eventually, I too was forced to join in the heinous chore of moving bodies from the gas chambers. It was terrible but it was the only way I had a chance to stay alive. I fought to stay sharp, always looking for a chance to rescue my sons. But I never had an opportunity.

Until one dark and rainy afternoon, however. I was ordered to go to Mengele's laboratory by one of his henchmen. I thought to myself this could be my chance! I'll attack the guard and take his gun! Get my boys and break away through the gates! Eagerly, I entered the building. But I froze when I saw a tangled pile of small, limp, motionless bodies." Boris's eyes began to tear up as he pushed onward.

"My heart began to pound like thunder, and my legs became weak as I realized that in that twisted pile of flesh, were my two little boys. They were cut to pieces and their eyes and teeth were gone! I lost my breath and I began to stagger and stumble, and I fainted as my legs gave out! But the guard began hitting me with his stick. I managed to stagger back up onto my feet as I felt my life draining from my body, and all that was left was my flesh and bones. I dredged up the strength to do what I had to do...to do what God forbid no parent should ever have to undertake, to care for their dead children.

Mengele then calmly entered the room.

"You see, I am a man of my word, Juda. You can have your boys back now. I am done with them!" and he hideously laughed at me.

My knees buckled again and I became dizzy as my world was spinning out of control, but I carefully picked up my two little boys and carried them away. I cried uncontrollably and spoke to them as I clutched them against my chest. 'No one can hurt you anymore my darling, beautiful little boys,' I cried to them.

I lurched and staggered, slipping in the mud as I headed back towards the crematorium. The rain was pouring heavily and we were soaking wet. I wailed at the top of my lungs,

"WHERE ARE YOU MY GOD?!!!" as I wept uncontrollably!

Everyone stopped and froze when they saw me carrying my two little boys.

Someone tried to help and take them from me... I don't know who it was, but I shouted through my tears;

"Get away! I will take care of my own blood!" When I entered the crematorium, the flames and the heat from the ovens were unbearable. My friend was stunned to see me carrying my two boys and he slowly opened the door to an oven. He said a prayer as I tenderly placed my sons inside. Maybe I too should have said a prayer, but who was listening for it?" Boris mournfully stated.

My father and I stood silently as this man revealed to us his horrific story. Maybe this was the first time he had ever told anyone about this tragedy, and he had kept it buried inside for so many years.

The recounting was very, very sad and difficult to hear. It became clear now why Boris was the way he was.

"I am so sorry for you, my friend. But how did you survive yourself?" my father asked.

"Determination! I made up my mind that I was not going to die until I could kill the maniac that brutally tortured and murdered my little boys. I came a long way to get here today. I traveled from South America to ask you and your boys a question," he said.

My father shrugged his shoulders.

"What is your question, Sir?"

Boris leaned forward to whisper something to us, when suddenly the doorbell jingled.

In walked a man wearing a loose trench coat and a dark brimmed hat. It was Mr. Kesh, a precious-gem dealer from India whom we had become close to.

"Good afternoon, Mr. Jacob, Mr. Joseph!" he exclaimed to us as he entered the store.

He was a short middle-aged man with jet black hair and a dark complexion, and he spoke with a very heavy Indian accent.

"I just want to show you some goods I brought back from South America, very nice, clean gems!" he stated.

Boris, who was waiting patiently, overheard Kesh mention South America, and that piqued his interest.

Immediately he started speaking Spanish to the salesman.

To our surprise the two were conversing in Spanish!

"Mr. Kesh, this is so strange to hear you speaking Spanish!" I exclaimed.

"Mr. Jacob, how do you say, 'You can't hit the home run if you don't have your stick!'" Kesh joked.

He explained that he needed to be well versed in languages to buy precious gemstones from around the world.

"In my school in Jaipur we were taught the language of many nations. It comes in handy when I travel to South America."

He reached into his trench coat, which concealed a black vest he was wearing with several large pockets. He removed a thin black pouch which contained dozens of tiny white envelopes.

Each one contained some sort of precious gem for sale.

It was typical for dealers to "wear" their goods like this, instead of keeping them in a briefcase, which could be snatched by a thief.

"Sorry, Mr. Kesh, this is a bad time for us. Can you come back later this week?" my father asked.

"I can come back, but only if you're going to buy something from me," he joked.

"Very well, see you sometime this week!" replied my father.

The salesman bid his farewells, "Goodbye, Mr. Jacob, Mr. Joseph. Adios, Mr. Boris," and he left the store.

It's funny how we refer to each other as "Mister" and seem to acquire an Indian accent ourselves, when Mr. Kesh is here.

My father locked the door and returned to our conversation with Boris.

"I'm sorry, sir. You were going to ask us a question," my father said.

Boris stared with his black empty eyes intently into my father's eyes.

"You people don't know me. I wouldn't expect you to go out on a limb for a stranger. You have a nice quiet business here, and it looks like you're doing pretty good. But there were millions of men, women and children that were murdered, and have no one to remember them. It is as if they never existed or they meant anything to anyone. There is no one to say kaddish for them, and no one to avenge their short-lived lives.

Meanwhile, Nazi murderers live all over South America, in plain sight. Living their lives in freedom with no remorse. Enjoying themselves, with no fear of retribution. To get to my point...I know where Joseph Mengele is hiding! And he has an army of his Nazi scum with him!

He is the beast, a bastard, and many other terrible things. But in truth, there is no foul word that can be contrived that does justice to what he is and what he has done.

I am here to ask you to help me kill that diabolical creature who tortured and killed my two little boys!" exclaimed Boris.

My father and I looked at each other as the man opened up his briefcase. It was filled with maps of South American towns and aerial pictures of a mountain.

"Believe me, I know where that piece of shit is. I have seen him, but he is well protected," Boris continued.

I expected my father to say,

"I'm sorry sir. We can't help you." But he seemed to hesitate.

Then, he spoke with compassion.

"Boris, I know how you felt when they tore your boys away from your arms. And I know how you felt when you didn't know what happened to your boys, and if you would ever see them again. And I even know how you felt when you believed your wife was dead. I have been there, my friend. But I can tell you, nothing is going to change if you kill that piece of shit!" stated my father.

Boris's face hardened and he became embittered.

"Yes, Watchmaker! Something will change! Justice will be served for my family, for all his victims, and for all of humanity!"

A single tear fell from his eye, and he wiped it with his sleeve.

My father looked up at the bell that hung from the door.

That bell was all we had left from our past.

He shook his head from left to right, pondering.

He reflected deeply about the situation.

Then, as if on cue, all the clocks in the store began to chime at once.

It was just as that horrible night when Wolfie and his henchmen raided our shop and killed my grandparents.

The blaring racket broke the silence as Boris waited for my father's decision.

It wasn't unusual for the clocks to chime all at once.

They do that every day, but this day was different.

It was as if there was some sort of a divine inference behind the deafening noise.

"Let me make a phone call. Could you come back in a few days?" my father asked.

Without saying another word, Boris abruptly gathered up his papers and returned them to his valise. He held up his big-fisted left hand and shook both our hands and gave me a small piece of paper with his hotel phone number on it.

As he turned to leave the store, I noticed the massive ugly scar on the back of his head which the Nazi's had inflicted on him. I walked with him to the door and I watched him as he disappeared into the crowded street, and it was closing time and so I locked the door.

"That was a sad story, Papa. If we hadn't been there ourselves, it would be difficult for anyone to believe what evil bastards those Nazi's and their collaborators were. But I hope he can move on and forget about killing Mengele, and let the Mossad take care of him," I stated.

My father did not reply right away, but I saw the look of determination on his face!

At once, I knew he was actually considering the mission.

"Are you mishugga, Papa?" I shouted.

"No, I'm not crazy. I'm just thinking about it," he said.

"I know when you are thinking about things, they generally come to be!" I exclaimed.

"Koby, look there is no question that many of those Nazi scoundrels escaped prosecution. They are living comfortably all over the world. What's so bad if we take a little trip to South America, and 'Benefit Humanity,' like Boris said."

"A little trip?! To Benefit Humanity?!! To kill a Nazi?!!!" I shouted.

"Good, I'm glad you understand," my father said facetiously.

"Now call Benny. We're going to need him," ordered my father.

"No, I'm not going to do it," I argued.

"Sooner or later he'll get caught! Let someone else put their neck on the line. It's too dangerous!" I shouted.

My father bowed his head.

"You don't understand what it feels like to have a child ripped away from you. To be powerless and unable to protect your family. To watch someone hurt your children, your family, and not be able to protect them, comfort them and heal them.

Boris is just one story. But there are hundreds of thousands of similar stories, including what happened to our own family. Those heartless Nazi bastards made sport of killing our people! Did you forget what happened to us at the airfield? They lined us up and made us into a shooting gallery game for their enjoyment!

At other camps they forced parents to watch as they murdered their children right in front of their eyes. They ripped babies away from their mothers and threw them up in the air for target practice! Did even one Nazi ever have compassion for our people?! No! They killed with a bloodthirsty lust!

And we were sitting pretty in America for the rest of the war, while our brothers and sisters were being murdered. With or without you, I'm going to South America. I'm going to take care of that Nazi son of a bitch and his army of sinister demon bastards!" my father ranted.

I hated it when he was always right.

I could see that he was determined to go, and I couldn't let him go without me.

I walked over to the phone and dialed Benny in Israel.

Sonia answered the phone and we spoke for several minutes.

She always invites me to come to Israel. She says she will introduce me to her gorgeous girlfriends and find me a wife.

"Those Israeli girls carry guns, and I'm afraid of them!" was my usual reply. But maybe someday I'll make the trip.

She informed me that Benny was out on a mission, but he calls her every night to check in.

She will tell him to get in touch with me.

And she ended our conversation with a "Shalom" and hung up.

"So, Papa, are you going to break out the guns and flame thrower?" I joked.

"Never mind, wise guy. We did a lot of damage for one man, two young boys and a little girl. For once, just stop complaining or I will leave you home and you will miss out on all the fun we are going to have," my father said.

We closed up shop and spoke very little on our way home. But we both knew once again that we were chosen to serve justice and retribution.

Chapter 3

That evening at 3 A.M. the phone in my room rang and startled me from my sound sleep.

I fumbled in the dark with the phone, It was Benny.

"Benny, you idiot, it's three in the morning here!" I scolded.

"Sorry about that, Koby. Sonia said you needed to talk to me right away, so here I am. What's going on? Is Papa all right?" Benny asked.

"Yes, he is fine. Okay, listen. Yesterday a man came to the shop. He was really in a bad way, a survivor from Krakow. He told us his horrendous story of how Mengele butchered his two little boys in Auschwitz. He claims to have information on Mengele's exact whereabouts and he wants us to go to South America and help kill him! After hearing the man's story, Papa is determined to go, but I'm trying to talk him out of it. The man says he absolutely knows where Mengele is, and that he has seen him. He has the maps and pictures to prove it. What do you think?" I sleepily stated.

There was silence for several seconds.

"I'm coming to see this guy. I'm leaving for the airport right   now!" Benny exclaimed.

"Bring me a falafel!" I joked as he hung up.

At breakfast that morning, I asked my father if he had heard the phone ringing in the middle of the night?

Hanna said she thought that it was the police calling on a possible burglary.

But when she heard me say, "Benny, you idiot!" she understood it was just Benny calling.

As for my father, he was having a bad dream when the phone call awoke him.

"I was dreaming about a German watch. It kept coming back for the same repair, over and over. But each time when I opened the watch case, red blood came pouring out of it!" my father stated.

"That sounds like a Holocaust dream," I remarked.

"You think so Einstein?" he sarcastically replied.

"So what did Benyamin have to say?" questioned my father.

"He wants to come and meet Boris," I replied.

"When did he say he is coming?" questioned my father.

"I think he was kidding, he said he was leaving immediately, but we probably won't see him for a month," I chuckled.

We finished our breakfast and dropped Hanna off at school before returning to the shop.

At the store that day there was an eerie feeling, almost like a dark cloud, lingered over us, as if something bad was going to happen.

I felt a little queasy and uneasy, as if I were going to the dentist for a root canal. That sort of feeling.

It was approximately 4 p.m. when someone abruptly pushed our door open, and knocked the bell off the door.

My father and I both ran from the back room to see what was happening.

And there was Benny, holding a crumpled paper bag, bending over and picking up the bell!

"You really need to find a way to keep this bell from falling off every time I open this door!" he complained.

"How about you enter the shop like a mensch, and it won't fall off!" my father kidded back.

We all hugged, and we were so happy to be together again!

"Holy shit! How did you get here so fast?" I said.

Benny reported,

"When I informed the prime minister of the urgency and importance of this meeting, they immediately put me on a private jet to New York. By the way, here is your falafel!"

I opened up the bag and found my crumpled up pita sandwich.

It was ice cold and soggy, but I was still going to eat it!

After catching up a bit, Benny had asked to meet Boris.

"Listen Benny, this Boris guy is a ticking time bomb. The story is that Mengele's henchmen tore his two little boys out from his defiant embrace a day after they arrived at Auschwitz. They gave him a chlami over the head and cracked his skull wide open, and only then were they able to extract his two twin little boys from him! They tossed him on a pile of dead bodies and mistook him for dead. Remarkably an old friend noticed him moving and schlepped him back to his barrack where he was able to recover. They put him to work in the crematorium where he was desperately contemplating how to rescue his two little ones from Mengele's grip. Then a few weeks later, Mengele had called Boris back to his slaughterhouse, taunting him specifically to reclaim his children. When he arrived there, he had a plan to take over the guards weapon and escape with his boys! However the blackest sky fell down upon him, when he saw that all that was left of his two little boys were their mutilated and twisted dead bodies. Mengele laughed as Boris wavered and staggered as he carried their bodies away, and returned to the crematorium where he then placed them in the raging ovens," I solemnly stated.

Benny shook his head in disbelief.

"If we weren't there to see things like that happening, I could never believe that kind of evil cruelty could exist, and how cold and heartless those Nazi son of a bitches were!" Benny said.

"And their collaborators too," I added.

Chapter 4

It was closing time and my father called Boris at his hotel. Boris asked my father if he had made his phone call.

My father replied,

"Yes, and there is someone here who wants to meet you."

"I'm on my way," Boris stated.

Meanwhile, Benny made himself at home and called Sonia.

They spoke for a few minutes and then began arguing in Hebrew. Then he abruptly hung up, but continued ranting to himself still in Hebrew.

"She says, when I get back to Israel, "WE" have to clean out the bomb shelter; the girls were playing and filled it with palm branches and rocks. But when she says "WE", that always means "ME!"," Benny complained.

After a short time, the bell on the door jingled and Boris entered the shop.

My father greeted him, and he placed the closed sign on the door and locked it behind him.

Benny put out his right hand to greet Boris.

But again the man had extended his left hand.

This caused Benny to reluctantly switch too, and they awkwardly shook with their left hands.

We were wondering about this odd practice, shaking left handedly. When we first met Boris he was holding his briefcase in his right hand.

I thought perhaps that was the reason, or possibly he was left-handed. It is very odd, but Boris is very complicated.

"I'm Benyamin, but you can call me Benny".

"I am Boris Wilensky. It's an honor to meet you, Sir." Boris replied.

"You know, when people greet each other it is uncommon to shake hands with the left," Benny stated, with his characteristic bluntness.

"Is that so?" Boris replied.

Benny raised his eyebrows and nodded his head.

"Benyamin, have you ever been to a Jewish funeral?" Boris continued.

"Yes, way too many," somberly replied Benny.

"So you are aware of the burial ritual in which friends and family of the deceased are each required to pick up a shovel and take a turn to cover the coffin with dirt, until the grave is completely filled? The reasoning is that we take care of our own to be assured it's done properly, we don't rely on strangers to indifferently and carelessly toss dirt on our loved ones, and hope it was done in a dignified and proper manner," paused Boris.

"It's considered the utmost final gift we can give to a loved one. However, first and foremost, when the shovel is first picked up, it is mandated that the spade of the shovel must be turned over, 'upside down' for the first few shovelfuls. Afterward the shovel should be turned back over and used the proper way.

It's difficult, of course, to pick up dirt that way. It's awkward, you have to balance the dirt on the back of the shovel, and it falls off, and not much can be moved. But it symbolizes that the death of a friend or loved one is also awkward and difficult. Life itself is out of balance, it's not right." Boris stared directly into Benny's eyes and continued.

"When I shake your hand with my left hand, that too is awkward and not right. The Germans murdered my wife and butchered my two little boys. Now, I too am awkward, not right and out of balance without them. I cry myself to sleep every night trying to understand how such cruelty could exist, and I relive those dreadful moments over and over and over in my mind.

I am that upside down shovel, trying to balance a horrific memory on my back, before I can turn over and try to be somewhat normal again, I have to do something. I have to avenge the deaths of my wife and children!"

Benny listened intently.

"I understand now," Benny mournfully stated and he nodded with respect.

"Koby says you have information on where Mengele is hiding. I am a General of the Mossad. If you know something, I can take that information back to Israel and we can look into it. If he is where you claim he is, we will get him and bring him back to Israel to stand trial. How does that sound to you?" Benny stated.

Boris stood there and his demeanor changed.

"No deal!!" he shouted, and started for the door.

"Wait a minute!" Benny shouted.

Boris stopped and hastily turned back towards us!

"I need to kill him myself! With my bare hands!! No ambushing and kidnapping to Israel! No trial! No other people involved! No one will even know except for us!" he stated.

"You yourself want to kill him?!!" exclaimed Benny.

"YES!!! With my bare hands!!" Boris shouted.

"He wants the four of us to go to South America and take out Mengele and the Nazi scumbags who are with him," I stated.

Benny scratched his head and thought for a moment, then replied,

"That would be extremely dangerous. These Nazis are smart. It would be difficult to get close to them. They're constantly looking out for any suspicious encounters. They live by the rule: kill or be killed. I know, I've hunted down many of these German bastards and they are all the same."

"If you are right and we can find Mengele, don't you think the world should share in knowledge that he was captured, tried and executed for what he did?" Benny questioned.

"No!!" countered Boris.

"Where was the world when WE were all getting murdered?!! We will know that he is finished! No one will ever know where he is or what we did with his body! There will be no making him a martyr! He will disappear with no one to mourn him, just like the victims he butchered! And I will be the one to do it! And when I kill him, it won't be a fast and easy death! Unlike the humane hanging he would get in Israel. No, I am going to take my time with that putrid maggot!" Boris ruthlessly stated.

Benny then turned to my father;

"Are you guys up for this?" he asked.

"Yes, I am full in!" declared my father.

I shook my head in disbelief.

"I can't believe I'm saying this, but I'm in too," I said.

"Okay Mr.Wilensky. It seems we have a deal. Now let's see what you have for information. Apparently you know more than the Mossad does," chuckled Benny.

Boris opened his briefcase. He removed a large map of Brazil and put it down on the glass showcase in front of us.

Benny immediately interjected.

"You don't know what you are talking about. Our sources say he is somewhere in Paraguay, not Brazil!"

"If your sources are so good, why didn't you catch him yourselves already?" Boris muttered.

Benny nodded reluctantly, and watched as Boris flattened out the map.

"This is the remote mountain area near Sao Paulo where Mengele has been hiding at his Uncle's Emerald mine. He goes by the name of 'Wolfgang Gerhard'," stated Boris.

"Another 'Wolfie!'" I interjected.

Boris then revealed several candid pictures of the mine, and a small fuzzy photograph of a dark-haired man with low dark eyebrows.

He was standing next to the large opening of a cave with a gang of Aryan looking guards, dressed in Nazi style uniforms, behind him.

"That's not enough. That picture is not clear," stated Benny.

Boris then arrogantly removed an 8x10 photograph from his briefcase, and handed it to Benny.

"Here is an enlargement, is this enough, Mr. General?" Boris sarcastically stated.

Benny scanned over the picture and handed it to my father, who in turn passed it to me.

"Do you see that gap between his front teeth?" Boris smugly questioned. Benny nodded.

"I'll never forget those black eyebrows and that space between his two front teeth!" Boris exclaimed.

"How did you get this picture and when was it taken?" questioned Benny.

"It was taken about two months ago. I obtained it from a close source," Boris replied.

"How did you find him? We have been looking for him for years with no luck?" Benny asked with astonishment.

"When my boys and I were taken to his laboratory, I noticed a guard staring at one of the scenic pictures of South America on the wall. Mengele mentioned to him that it was his Uncle's Emerald mine in Sao Paulo, Brazil. Mengele showed him his ring with a large Emerald, presumably from the mine.

I felt sooner or later he would show up there, since he had no money. It was the only place he could hide out for free," Boris stated.

"Okay, Mr. Wilensky, assuming that's so, the Brazilian military and local authorities are not going to let us just walk into town and take him out for a joy ride. Do you have anyone who can help us down there?" Benny asked.

"No, but I have a small villa close by, where I have been living for the past eight years," he said.

"You've been watching that mine for the past eight years?" I asked.

"Yes, and he finally showed up there about six months ago. How does it go? 'The rat will always return to its nest!'" replied Boris.

"One thing for sure," he continued. "It will take an army to get into the mine complex. It is heavily guarded, and he is always surrounded by his bodyguards. You're right; the local government protects them too, since the mine pays off many of the local politicians."

"Do you know how they market their gemstones?" my father questioned.

"Yes. They have a building where the stones are sorted and polished. I know of a local jeweler who often goes to the mine to buy gemstones. He is friendly with them, and they know him. He is the one who gave me this picture," replied Boris.

"I have an idea! If we can pose as buyers from America, it may be a way to get into the place," my father suggested.

"Right! Hey, Mengele, we four Jewish survivors are here to buy some of your blood Emeralds. How about letting us in so we can kill you?" I sarcastically stated.

Just then there was a knock on the door.

"We're closed!" my father shouted.

But the knocking persisted. I went to the front door to see who it was.

"Mr. Kesh! You're too late. We're closed," I firmly stated.

"This is my last stop. If I don't see you today it will have to be next week and you will have last picks on my goods!" he shot back.

I reluctantly let him in, and he followed me to the back of the store where the others were quietly talking.

"Mr. Benny! When did you get here?" Kesh exclaimed.

"Just a little while ago, Mr.Kesh," he replied.

I glanced at my father and I could see his gears turning.

"Mr. Kesh, do you remember Mr. Boris from the other day?" my father asked.

"Yes, how are you today, Mr. Boris?" Kesh replied.

Boris shook his head. But he was anxious for Kesh to leave.

"Mr. Kesh, Boris has knowledge of a mine in Brazil that has the finest Emeralds. They are selling AAA gem quality polished Emeralds for pennies on the dollar. They hit a major vein of beryl and they are looking to move their inventory. It looks like it could be a very lucrative venture. We are thinking about taking a trip down to the mine and buying a truck load of Emeralds," my father stated.

"Oh, Mr. Joseph. Emeralds are on da rise. Dat would be a very smart ting you know, if you could do dat," he said with his heavy Indian accent.

"There is one little problem," my father continued.

"They are very careful who they let in and we don't have any connections to make an introduction. Do you have a reference we could use?" my father asked.

"Tell me where the mine is and I'll make a few phone calls," Kesh deviously said.

"It's in the Sao Paulo area," replied Boris.

Kesh thought about it for a moment.

"I have been to that region. There is the Jacupiranga Mine, which I have been to many times. Dey don't have doze Emeralds, but they do have a good variety of semi-precious stones like Peridot and Aquamarine. I know da owner very well. Let me call da guy and I will let you know. In the meantime, let me show you some beautiful Burmese rubies and Ceylon sapphires that I picked up for a very good price!" Kesh exclaimed.

"I don't think we need any of those. I still have the last parcels you sold us," I replied.

"Never mind Koby, let's take a look. Mr. Kesh came all the way out here," my father said, as he winked at me.

After about an hour of painfully listening to my father haggling with Kesh, we were all mentally drained and delusional.

My father was purchasing about $5,000 worth of gems we didn't even need, mostly to butter up Kesh for helping us get into the mine, but also just to get rid of him.

You see, just telling Kesh "No" to an item he is trying to sell you such as a diamond or other precious stone, doesn't work with Kesh. You have to say "No!" ten times and then it's on to the next item or it goes into his "Maybe pile".

From there you have to say "No!" another ten times and so it goes!

If you waiver off course, and stumble for an instant and show a bit of interest in a gem, it can be tragic.

Kesh can be extremely persistent until he gets all of your money.

My father finally took out our checkbook to pay for the items, and as he began to write the check, Kesh snatched the pen out of his hand!

"Wait! I have something else to show you Mr. Joseph!" he exclaimed.

He reached into his vest and took out a small black ring box. He delicately held it as he carefully opened it, revealing a large oval shaped blood red stone set into a large men's gold ring.

"I don't need another ruby ring!" my father stated.

"Ah, dis is not a ruby, Mr. Joseph. Dis is a Red Diamond! You will never see another one of dese! It is da most rare of all diamonds!" salivated Kesh.

We all gathered around closer to see the jewel.

"How big is it?" I asked.

"Approximately five and a half carats, Mr. Jacob!" he replied.

My father picked it up, rotated it and looked at it under his jeweler's loupe. He passed it to me and I too used his loupe and rotated it in the light and examined the stone.

"It's almost flawless, Mr. Joseph," Kesh exclaimed.

"How much do you want for it?" my father questioned in a seemingly uninterested manner as to appear to Kesh that he had no desire or interest to purchase the diamond.

The salesman began calculating numbers in his head and replied;

"Only $75,200.00, Mr. Joseph".

"Holy shit! We have so many diamonds, Papa. We don't need another diamond, even if it is a rare red diamond!" I exclaimed.

"How about $70,000?" my father offered as he totally ignored my plea to restrain himself.

"Oh Mr. Joseph, look how beautiful dis diamond is. You will never see another one like dis. I assure you, it's a very good price. Da best I can do is $75,000" Mr. Kesh countered.

"Oh gee, thanks, Kesh, you only took off 200 dollars. Papa you are not really considering this are you?" I exclaimed with dire frustration.

"$72,000!" my father countered back.

"Mr. Joseph, I gave you a very good price. But if you pay me cash I can go down to $74,800" Kesh offered.

I stood there frozen as I watched this haggling match go back and forth between these two cunning sharks.

"$72,500 and I'll also buy the parcels I was originally going to buy," my father counter offered.

"What do you mean, Mr. Joseph? Doze were a done deal!" exclaimed Kesh.

"It was a done deal until you pulled the pen from my hand and stopped me from writing the check!" replied my father.

"$72,500 for the Red Diamond and $4,000 for the rubies and sapphires make $76,500" my father insisted, and he held out his hand to shake and close the deal.

"Mr. Joseph, we already agreed on $5,000 for da rubies and sapphires!" exclaimed Kesh.

"Once again, that was before you pulled the pen from my hand!" argued my father.

We watched intently as the two men bargained back and forth for the high value jewels.

My father calmly sat there, still with his empty hand reaching out.

"Deal?" my father questioned and he continued to offer his hand.

Kesh was frustrated. He had backed himself into a corner. If he didn't accept the offer for the red diamond, rubies and sapphires, they would go back in his pocket and he would leave with nothing. If he took the offer, he would be making less on all the gems but still a hefty profit.

"Mr. Joseph, when I go to da other merchants dey pay what I ask without all dis bargaining!" pleaded Kesh.

"But you know that I do bargain. And I know you raise the prices to adjust for that!" stated my father.

"Okay, but I didn't tink you were going to beat me up so badly on dis one," Kesh replied.

"$76,000, Mr.Kesh" my father repeated.

"You said $76,500 before!" exclaimed Kesh.

"Okay $76,500 it is!" and my father grabbed the salesman's hand and they shook to seal the deal.

My father took his pen back from Kesh and began to write the check once again.

"Wait Mr. Joseph! I thought you were going to pay me cash!" exclaimed Kesh.

"No. You asked for cash but I never agreed to it," my father replied, and he continued to write out the check.

He tore it from his ledger book and handed it over to Kesh.

"You know, Mr. Joseph, I never get headaches, but today you gave me a big one!" Kesh joked.

"Okay, don't forget to let me know about that mine in Brazil. I'll be waiting to hear from you," my father reiterated.

Kesh quickly gathered his belongings and double-checked to see if he had missed or dropped any gems.

He seemed to be in a rush and with his typical flourish he said,

"Tank you Mr. Joseph, Mr. Jacob. Nice to see you again, Mr. Benny and adios, Mr. Boris," and he tucked the check away into a certain zippered pocket in his vest and abruptly headed toward the door.

I walked with him to the front, unlocked the door and watched him swiftly walk down the street to his next unsuspecting victim.

When I returned to the back of the store, Benny was joking about how father actually got the better of Kesh.

"That was crazy, Papa! You never cease to amaze me!" Benny exclaimed.

"You are the master of negotiation, Papa!" I added.

"Mr. Kesh is a nice man, but I'm not like the other putz jewelers he sells to," claimed my father.

"Gentlemen, whether you think so or not, the man from India played you the entire time. Right now he is calling his wife to tell her how he suckered you!" Boris stated as he voiced his opinion.

He seemed to have found the entire exchange interesting but predictable.

"I'm tired and it's getting late, and I would like to go back to my hotel."

"I'm sorry to have kept you here so long, it is late," my father acknowledged.

"I'll be in contact with you when I hear back from Kesh. In the meantime, Benny get in touch with your people. Figure out a way to get us supplies and have them dropped to Boris's villa. We're going to need some serious firepower and lots of agents to take on those Nazi bastards," my father stated.

"No!! I told you we have to do this alone! If you bring in Mossad, they will take over, and bring him back to Israel!" Boris shouted.

"Okay, okay we'll do it your way, but I may need a little help!" exclaimed Benny.

Boris settled down and acknowledged that a little help would be okay.

As I walked Boris to the door, I told him I was worried.

"This is going to be very dangerous," I nervously stated.

"For you three, this will be easy compared to what you did in Poland," Boris replied.

He swiftly walked out the door, and again I noticed the large gaping scar on the back of his head.

I continued watching him as he disappeared down the busy street. But I couldn't imagine how he was able to carry on each day, with that constant reminder of his children's murder on the back of his head.

I rejoined Benny and my father as they were still chatting in the back room.

"Gee, what a downer Boris is!" Benny complained.

"Papa, do you really think Kesh took advantage of you? Like Boris said," I questioned.

"That guy doesn't know dreck. Did you see the look on Kesh's face when I told him he canceled the deal by pulling the pen from my hand! So what do you think, Benny? Did he cheat me or did I cheat him?" my father inquired.

"What do I think? I think I'm so hungry I could eat frogs!" he joked.

"You're right! Let's go to Chinatown and eat some Chinese food! Which just so happens to be my favorite reason for coming to America! And Koby you have to pay. I don't have any money left," chuckled my father.

We closed up the store, and the three of us left for Chinatown.

Chapter 5

A few days later in our shop, we were helping several customers when Kesh returned.

The store was very busy, and it was proper for vendors to just wait their turn quietly until we had some time for them. Taking care of customers was always a priority.

He stood in the corner with his hands clasped together, trying to be patient, checking his watch every few minutes.

After I finished changing the time on an elderly woman's watch, I was finally available.

"Can you use anything today, Mr. Jacob?" Kesh secretly whispered, as not to draw any public attention towards him. He was always concerned that he was a precious gems dealer and a target for robbery once he left the store.

"After the beating you gave our bank account the other night, I don't think we're buying anything today," I whispered back.

"Is your father here? I need to speak to both of you," he softly stated.

I brought Kesh back to the repair shop, where my father was working, and when my father noticed us he wiped his hands off on an old towel, as he stood up from his workbench.

"What's the good word, Mr. Kesh?" he asked.

"Apparently Emeralds is da good word, Mr. Joseph. I contacted my friends at da Jacupiranga mine. Dey know the owner of da Emerald mine and it's not too far from dem. He said the guy is a German," stated Kesh.

My father ignorantly addressed me.

"Koby, did you hear anything about a German?" questioned my father.

"Uhhh, no but who cares who owns it as long as the prices are right!" I responded indifferently.

"Okay, here's the ting. My friends say dey don't know you, so dey can't provide an introduction, but if I go with you, dey'll do it!" stated Kesh.

"Oh, no, Mr. Kesh, that's a bad idea. We don't want to put you out like that. Tell your friends I'll send them $1,000 for the introduction," insisted my father.

Kesh persisted...

"Da problem is dey won't do it unless I go too. It's a big deal to recommend someone down dere. If dey don't know you, why would they put der reputation on da line? So eider I go wid you, or I'll go myself and sell you some gorgeous green Emeralds when I get back!" Kesh flatly stated.

"Let me talk to my father a minute, Mr.Kesh."

He left the room and I closed the door behind him.

"There's no way we can get Kesh involved in this! He doesn't have a clue why we're really going down there. He could get killed!" I exclaimed.

"Never mind! Once we get down there and we have the introduction, we'll leave him at the hotel until we are finished with Mengele. I'll make sure he stays safe," my father replied.

I shook my head in disbelief, then I opened the door and called Kesh back in.

"It looks like we have a deal, Mr. Kesh! But I think it would be better for all of us to act as one buyer. We can sort out the merchandise when we get back to America. Agreed?” stated my father.

“Agreed, and it’s already set. Da introduction was made a few days ago,” replied Kesh.

“How soon before we leave?” I asked him.

“We’re leaving in five weeks,” he jovially replied.

“I have August 2nd to da 5th available. I already had my ticket, since I was planning to go to South America anyway. Most jewelers close August for da summer vacation. I know you do, too. So I already booked da flights for da both you on Pan Am. No smoking right?” Kesh confidently stated.

My father and I looked at each other and shrugged our shoulders.

“Okay, but I get the window seat!” I joked.

“Mr. Kesh, are you sure your man can get us into the Emerald mine?” my father questioned.

“Very sure, Mr. Joseph. It’s all set. How do you like that for service! I already called dem and dey are excited to see us. Da mine owner is sending someone to pick us up at the airport. And we are invited to stay with him at his villa near da mine!” he enthusiastically stated.

Upon hearing this, my father and I were in a state of shock, but we tried to remain calm.

“You know, I actually met him once at a gem show in Brazil,” Kesh added.

“What do you know about him?” my father questioned.

“Very little, but I was told they came to Brazil before da war. Dey refused to join the Nazis so they fled da country. Dey were lucky to escape. If dey were caught trying to leave, dey would have been arrested and trown into the prison!” Kesh exclaimed.

“Mr. Kesh do you know what the Emerald mine owner’s name is?” my father coyly asked.

"You know, it's funny, but I only know his first name. It's Albert. I tink he lives there with his cousin, who was a doctor from Germany.

"All right, Mr. Kesh, we have a lot of planning to do. I'm sure we'll see you in the following weeks," my father concluded.

Ever persistent, Kesh asked,

"Are you sure you couldn't use a few more tings. I have some beautiful pearls from da South Seas!"

"Goodbye, Mr.Kesh," I said emphatically, and I walked him to the door.

Chapter 6

"**W**here is Benyamin?!" my father shouted from the repair shop.

"He went to Macy's to buy some clothes for his kids. He should be back soon," I replied.

"Call Boris. We need to have a meeting tonight!" my father ordered.

A few minutes later Benny pushed the front door open with his back, while several large shopping bags occupied his hands.

"Hurry up! Get in here, Benny!" my father shouted.

"Kesh was here. He secured our pass into the mine, but he said his connection wouldn't do it unless we agreed that he was to accompany us," I reported.

"I'm not surprised. He probably couldn't sleep at night, knowing we would be out there buying gems from someone else. He must have finagled some sort of kick back from them, and wanted to be there to make sure he doesn't get cheated out of it," declared Benny.

"There's more. Mengele's cousin Albert owns the mine, and Mengele is down there with him! Kesh had met him at a gem show in Brazil sometime ago. Albert told him some bullshit story that they left Germany before the war started because they wouldn't raise their hands to Hitler!" I ridiculously stated.

"You're kidding me!" Benny exclaimed.

"There's more! Kesh had already reserved our plane tickets, and Papa and I are leaving for Brazil August 2nd along with Kesh on the very same flight. Then, they're picking us up at the airport, and we're invited to stay at Albert's villa!" I exclaimed.

Benny stood there in amazement.

Then he squeezed his face with his hands, while staring at the floor. He shook his head from left to right and began whispering to himself in Hebrew.

"Moqesh, moqesh, moqesh, moqesh, moqesh!" he mumbled, each word getting louder than the last.

"What's the matter?" my father questioned.

"IT'S A TRAP!" Benny shouted.

"Don't you think it's incredible that Kesh just happens to get us passage into the mine where Mengele is hiding?

And they are picking you up from the airport! And you have a special invitation to stay at their villa! This is absolutely a trap!" Benny exclaimed.

"I agree! Kesh is setting us up! He must have told them about us, and they bribed him to help get us there. Okay, Papa, we're not going! Benny is right. This is too freaky!" I exclaimed.

"No, absolutely we are going! If these Nazi scum know about us, they probably know where we live too. Someday they could send some thugs to New York to kill us right here in our store! No, we are not going to live like that, my boy. We're going to Brazil and take the fight to them and finish off these blood sucking bastards once and for all!" my father insisted.

"I think they may be looking for some sort of personal revenge. It could have been in the making for quite some time," Benny added.

My father continued,

"Okay Benyamin, we know we are the only ones we can trust. We don't give any details about our plans to Kesh. We'll need back up. More Mossad agents, and guns with plenty of ammunition that we can access after we land in Brazil," commanded my father.

"Papa, I know you are used to being in charge," Benny protested. "But I am a general in the Mossad, for god sakes! Let me come up with the plan!"

My father folded his arms and stood there;

"Okay, what's your big plan, Mr. General?" my father sarcastically stated.

"First, we don't tell Kesh what we're up to. We can't trust him. Next I'll get in touch with my agents in Israel for back up. Third, I'll coordinate the guns and ammunition to be sent to us in Brazil!"

My father rolled his eyes and collapsed into his chair!

"Benny, what about your promise to Boris? No others involved," I professed.

"Never mind Boris, I'll keep it small with just a few agents to help out. Besides as long as he gets to kill Mengele, that should keep him happy," declared Benny.

Benny then walked to the phone and called Sonia. They spoke briefly and it didn't seem to have anything to do with "Cleaning out the bunker," but rather serious business.

He informed us he was flying back to Israel to get the team organized and to get the preparations in place.

We decided it would be best if we flew down a day earlier rather than at the same time as Kesh, when we would be expected.

I called Kesh and informed him that we had a family event to attend on the August 2nd date, but would meet him there the day after on the 3rd of August.

Upon hearing of this change, Kesh became very upset and stated that if we did not all arrive together, they might not allow us into the mine.

I told him we would meet him there and not to worry, since they wanted our American money.

He also insisted that Benny should join us, since he was still part owner of the store, and the mine owners expected to meet "all" of the store owners.

"They could be offended and not give us "The best deals" if Benny doesn't show up," he threatened.

I told him that Benny was in Israel taking it easy, and it would be impossible to get him there, since he was a family man now and had little to do with the store. But he would be there in spirit.

Kesh then insisted on still picking us up from the airport with a driver from the mine, and so we agreed to that.

I gave him the flight information, and that the plane was scheduled to arrive at about 7 o'clock in the evening.

He didn't seem happy about the changes we made, but he had no choice.

After I hung up, I thought it seemed odd that Kesh was so concerned about the details of us getting there.

Maybe it is a trap, and he is in on it. No, it's impossible. We have known Mr. Kesh for many years, and besides doing business with him he was almost a part of our family.

My father contacted his friend Fritz, the German pilot who had flown us out of Poland, and he coordinated with him to pick us up at the Sao Paulo airport at midnight, August 3rd, and to fly us back to New York.

We knew it would be difficult to catch a flight on a regular passenger airline, especially if we were rushing to leave the country after a fierce gunfight at the mine.

It seemed that Kesh was definitely up to something. Although, knowing Kesh, he may have realistically been concerned about buying Emeralds for the cheapest price possible.

Chapter 7

As the days marched on, we were in constant contact with Benny every day.

The plan was that he would arrive a few weeks before we would arrive, and would do surveillance and prepare for the attack.

He's going to meet us at the airport and bring us to Boris's villa, where we will solidify plans and collect our weapons.

As we prepared for our mission, we made provisions for Hanna.

In the event our mission failed and we didn't come back, she was to stay with a close relative's family.

Papa wrote a letter to her, explaining to her why we had to go, and that he left everything we had to her in the unfortunate event that we did not return, and so he left it in the cookie jar in our kitchen.

We had packed lightly and my father decided not to bring a bankroll of money.

After all, we really weren't going there to buy anything, and he didn't want our money to end up in the wrong hands should things not go our way. But oddly he chose to wear that men's ring, the one set with the large red diamond that he had brought from Kesh.

He removed it from the safe and put it on.

"Why are you bringing that?" I questioned.

"I don't know, but I have a feeling I should wear it. Maybe it will be lucky," he replied.

Chapter 8

August 2nd quickly arrived and we were anxious to get to Brazil. Our bags were packed and ready to go. All that was left was our passports and a lot of luck.

My father and I carried our small suitcases to the taxi which had just arrived and was taking us to the airport.

Hanna was getting picked up after we left, and will be staying with a friend of hers for the week.

My stomach always begins to feel nauseous when I think of being on a plane.

I think it's a conditioned response to the extreme airsickness I experienced from when we had that hard landing in Sweden.

I silently sat in the back seat of the taxi cab watching all the cars go by us. Everyone was going somewhere.

They seemed not to have a worry in the world, as my heart began to race and I started to feel queasy. Why are we doing this crazy thing? We could get ourselves killed over a total stranger's obsession.

I knew it would be useless to try just one more time to talk my father out of this crazy endeavor.

So I just sat there, wishing we were going somewhere else.

The cab dropped us off at the Pan Am terminal and we made our way to the security gate.

An armed security guard asked us why we were traveling to Brazil, and that question caught me off guard.

I wanted to reply;

"We are on a crazy mission to kill the evil Nazi, Joseph Mengele. Please don't let us on the plane!"

But my father quickly said we were going "to take care of someone in Sao Paulo," and he winked at me.

I began to nervously laugh.

Maybe it was a release of my built-up stress, or maybe it was my reaction to my father's clever remark.

At any rate, I began to feel more at ease since my father was with me.

Because of his strength, I felt we were going to be alright.

We boarded the plane and found our seats near the front of the plane.

Given that there were a lot of empty seats, I was surprised that a man was sitting in our row, next to the window.

Knowing that my father preferred the aisle, I sat down next to the man.

He was of medium size build, approximately 40 years old, wearing a black business suit, with perfectly slicked down blond hair and heavy black-framed glasses.

"Good morning," I said.

He nodded and replied back to me in German,

"Danke."

Maybe I was being paranoid, but as far as I was concerned, any German was a Nazi in disguise!

I nudged my father with my elbow and whispered into his ear.

"There's a Nazi sitting next to me!"

He leaned forward and glanced at the man, shrugged his shoulders and began reading his newspaper.

I tried to make a little small talk with the man, but it was apparent he was avoiding eye contact with me, and was not interested in conversation.

As the plane prepared for takeoff, I started once again to feel uneasy.

I prayed that I would not have to go through another landing like the one in Sweden.

The engines suddenly accelerated and the jet began to quickly taxi down the runway.

The jet plane was quickly picking up speed, and began to vigorously shake and rumble as it accelerated, and then suddenly it got quiet as we became airborne.

After about an hour, the man sitting next to me nudged me and politely stated that he had to use the restroom.

My father and I moved out of our seats so he could get by.

I whispered to my father that the man reminded me of Wolfie, and that he could really be a Nazi!

My father thought I was being overly suspicious and paranoid.

A few minutes later the man returned back to his seat.

He was now wearing a white short sleeved shirt, after having removed his jacket and tie in the restroom.

He reached up into the overhead compartment and neatly tucked the garments into his carry on suitcase.

He then stood there and waited patiently, as my father and I got up again so that he could return to his window seat.

As he brushed by me, I noticed a dark insignia under his armpit, which was vaguely visible through his thin cotton shirt.

"It could be a swastika!" I thought, remembering that most Nazi officers had such a tattoo in the same spot.

"Dad! I think I saw a swastika tattoo through his shirt!" I emphatically whispered.

My father still did not appear to be concerned.

He whispered back that I should get a better look, when I had the chance, maybe it was just a dark mole.

"Is it a coincidence that we have a Nazi bastard sitting next to me!" I whispered, in alarm.

My father nodded his head "yes" and went back to reading his newspaper.

We continued to fly on, and I waited impatiently for this man to fall asleep or move in a way that I could get a better look at what was under his shirt.

With about two hours remaining on the flight, the German began getting restless.

Once again he motioned to me that he had to go to the restroom.

I jumped up and "accidentally" lifted his shirt, exposing his skin for a moment.

I wanted my father to see if there was an incriminating tattoo.

The man gave me a dirty look and I apologized, and he then proceeded on to the restroom.

When I sat back down I exclaimed to my father,

"Well! What did you see?!"

"I saw a small black swastika," he admitted.

Nevertheless, he did not seem upset. While I started to panic and break out into a cold sweat.

"What are we going to do now? This bastard must be a plant to kill us!" I cried.

"Switch seats with me, I want to see what his intentions are. One thing I learned about Nazis, they don't like being out of control," my father stated.

We quickly changed seats and moments later the German returned.

He made an awkward face, when he realized that my father was now going to be sitting next to him, and I was in the aisle seat.

It was clear that he was uncomfortable sitting next to my father.

A stewardess approached us and asked if we needed anything.

The man asked for a large German beer, and she responded that she would return with it shortly.

"Koby, I should have asked the stewardess for a blanket. Go ask her for one, and be kind enough to get the beer for our friend here," my father said.

I hopped out of my seat and caught up to the stewardess at the canteen station.

When I returned with the blanket and a large foaming glass of beer, the man looked unpleasantly surprised.

I held onto the blanket, as I passed the glass of beer to my father who then passed it onto the German.

"Enjoy your beer, Herr Unteroffizier. You know, we once served a select group of German officers the same sort of beer in a bar in Stockholm about 10 years ago," jeered my father.

The man's face grew stern and he stared into his drink.

"Go ahead, drink up friend," my father egged him on.

The man stared into his drink, but refused to raise his glass.

"Is there something wrong with your beer?" my father asked.

It was obvious he had hit a chord with the Nazi, who somehow was aware of the poisoned beer Benny had served to the Nazi officers at the bar in Stockholm.

Believing he too may have been given a poisoned brew, he reacted and threw the beer at my father!

Then the German lunged at him with a switchblade knife he had concealed in his pocket. However, before he could stab his blade, my father turned sideways and took hold of his knife wielding arm and viciously elbowed the

Nazi three times into his throat, crushing his wind pipe as he pinned the man down against the window!

The Nazi with his wildly bulging eyes, thrashed about for a few seconds, gasping for air, but my father's blows were lethal.

My father firmly held his hand over the man's mouth to keep him silent.

"Shhhh, Sie mussen sterben leise (You must die quietly), Herr Unteroffizier. In a moment you will be reunited with your Nazi swine in the smoldering tar pits of hell!" my father whispered into his ear.

Quickly, I concealed him from view with the blanket.

When he finally stopped thrashing about, we covered his body to make it look as if he was asleep.

My father quickly straightened out the area, and I got up to see if anyone had noticed the ruckus.

A woman sitting two rows behind us asked if everything was okay. I told her that the passenger next to the window was airsick and had thrown up beer all over my father.

She made a look of disgust and shrunk back to avoid any stray vomit that might be lurking her way.

My father began rummaging through the German's pockets. And he indeed found a billfold that contained a photograph of my father and me.

"Are you okay, Papa?" I exclaimed.

"I'm fine, but we will have to make a run for it when the plane lands," he whispered.

"Papa, you referred to him as an Unteroffizier, what did that mean?" I quietly asked.

"The lowest rank given to a Nazi officer, is an 'Under Officer,' I thought he would have been surely offended that I insulted him and under-ranked him. Especially if he felt he was an esteemed bastard.

Either way I got his goat," replied my father.

"If this Nazi was following us. There could be more on this plane and in the airport. When we land, we have to watch our backs and get the hell out of there," he continued.

Chapter 9

It wasn't long before the plane began making its gradual descent to Araraquara, Brazil.

When it finally touched down and landed we bolted for the door and rushed to exit. Benny was already at the gate and waiting for us.

"What happened to you, Papa? Did you pee all over yourself?" he joked, after seeing my father's wet clothes.

"There was a Nazi planted next to us on the plane, and he couldn't hold his liquor. Let's quickly get out of here before they discover his untimely demise and we have any more surprises!" I stated.

As we exited the airport we were extremely nervous and we were trying to determine how it was that the Nazi knew what day and flight we would be embarking on to Brazil. We quickly got into Benny's car and sped off!

"How do you suppose that Nazi planted himself next to us with no knowledge of our transportation plans?" I questioned.

"The only person who knew your flight information was Kesh. But he thought you were arriving a day later. They must have been following you. That's what I would have done," responded Benny.

After driving down miles of dilapidated bumpy gravel roads which were riddled with potholes, we finally turned into a long jungle-lined driveway, which ended at a small remote farm.

"So this is Boris's villa? It sounded more glamorous than it actually is," I disappointedly stated.

The air that night was so hot we were relieved to finally get out of the car.

"Who's in the house, Benny?" my father questioned.

"My best agent, and Boris," replied Benny.

"How many men did you bring?" my father asked.

"Two, well actually one man and a woman," replied Benny.

"That's all! There are only three of you!" my father shouted, throwing up his hands.

"Papa, Boris was severely against me bringing in a crew of agents. Remember that Cowboy Sergeant at the Embassy in Stockholm? He was a Texas Ranger. Remember his expression, 'One Riot, One Ranger?' Well we're like that too. We are the Israeli Mossad. One of us can do a lot of devastation! Don't worry, besides I have you two as well!" Benny confidently stated.

He pulled open the old screen door that led into the villa, and we followed him in as the door slammed behind us.

It was even hotter inside the house than it had been inside the car.

The villa was impoverished, and populated with dozens of large black flies aimlessly buzzing all around the light fixture which was hanging down from an antiquated ceiling fan that was spinning out of balance, and was merely circulating the hot air.

Boris was at the kitchen table, peeling an apple when we walked into his home.

He stood up, and again he kept up his awkward practice of greeting us with his left hand.

Then he sat back down and continued peeling his apple without breaking the trail of the apple's skin...just one long peel from beginning to end. Then he greeted us by saying;

"Welcome to my hell."

"Where are the other agents?" I asked.

"One is developing pictures in the barn. We've been watching the mine and taking telescopic photographs. I think you will be surprised at what we found," Benny stated.

Just then we heard a woman's voice singing outside in the yard and heading towards the house.

The screen door creaked open and a beautiful blond woman was standing there with a hand full of black and white photographs.

"Sonya! What are you doing here?!" I exclaimed, as we raced over to greet her.

"It's so good to see you two! I wish the girls were here too, but under the circumstances I had to leave them on the kibbutz," she stated.

"Benny, why is Sonya here? This is too dangerous for her!" I shouted.

"Relax, Koby," he replied.

"I told you I was bringing my best agents. And she is the best."

"Where is the other agent?" I asked.

"He is dressed up as a banana tree, watching the mine from the jungle."

Benny took the pictures from his wife and spread them all around the table.

There were many photos of two men and groups of guards.

"Most of these guards I don't recognize from my database. But these two men, I do know. This one is Mengele's cousin, Albert Heim, whose father Adolf originally owned the mine. He was killed in an undisclosed place during the war, and now Albert runs the mine. Albert, in his own right was also a very loathsome Nazi too. He was vicious like his cousin Mengele. He brutally tortured his victims to death at the Mauthausen camp in Austria.

Heim carried on much like Mengele. Often he would operate on prisoners with no anesthesia, and inject lethal poisons into their veins. He was known to heinously cut open his victims' chests and pull their hearts out while they were awake. They referred to him as 'Dr. Death,'" Benny proclaimed.

"This other picture is of Mengele. Boris was correct with his surveillance," Benny commended.

Upon hearing that compliment, Boris stood up and took a ceremonious bow.

"He lives here now and works closely with his cousin, Albert.

As we all know, Mengele did his savagery at the Auschwitz concentration camp," continued Benny.

I never understood why they called those evil sites "camps". To my understanding a camp was a fun place to go when you are on summer holiday. These places were filled with horror and death. "Concentration Hell Holes" would have been a better-suited name.

"Finsters mir! The two most evil demons together!" exclaimed my father.

"Yes, the darkness has fallen over all of us. 'The Angel of Death' and 'Dr. Death'" I nervously stated.

"These two plagues have been hiding here, while the whole world has been over turning fiery brimstone searching for these two demons. God chose us to pass judgment on them. We'll put them on trial ourselves, and execute them in our own way to avenge the heinous torturous deaths they performed on so many!" Benny raged.

"Remember! Mengele is mine," Boris interjected.

"I don't want you messing things up Boris. You are a civilian with a lot of emotional baggage. I'll send for you when we are ready to dispatch Mengele," replied Benny.

I thought that was an interesting way to phrase killing one of the most evil men in the world.

To have him "dispatched," as if he were a piece of toilet paper being flushed down the toilet. How appropriate, I thought to myself.

Everyone was on edge and the heat was oppressive.

My father was anxious to view the mine and do some of his own surveillance.

Benny decided it would be best if we waited until later in the night, before we made our way over.

While we waited, my father asked where the cache of weapons was.

"I have a surprise for you, Papa," Benny stated.

He reached into a closet and removed two short rifles.

"This is the newest Israeli-made machine gun. It's a prototype and it's not yet available to anyone but the Mossad.

It's called an Uzi. My friend Uziel invented it, and he wanted you and Koby to have one!" Benny exclaimed.

"Tell your friend I will honor him and kill many Nazi sons of bitches with his gun!" my father declared.

"This machine gun is all you will need," Benny stated confidently.

The moon was bright and we began our long journey through the jungle to the mine.

Boris stayed behind with Sonya, not wanting to make the long hike.

It took us about an hour of stumbling through the jungle undergrowth, and it reminded me of our time in the woods in Poland.

Except this time, I was more concerned about poisonous spiders and venomous snakes lurking on the jungle floor than Nazi's.

When we finally arrived at the outskirts of the mine, we were positioned at the peak of a mountainous hill, and were looking down at the site of the mine. It was brightly illuminated and the entire grounds were covered with crushed white gravel.

The site was considerably a large area of approximately 5 acres, and they had erected a classic concentration camp style electric fence, which surrounded the perimeter.

The entrance to the mine itself was dug into the side of a hill at the opposite edge of the property, and guards, dressed as German soldiers were carrying rifles, and patrolling over the area.

A small trolley track led into the entrance of the mine, and a line of metal dump carts sat idly on them.

The following day they would be used to dump their pay dirt onto a conveyor belt which led to an enormous rock crushing machine.

Then the dump carts would be returned back into the depths of the mine to continue the process. We heard a rustling in the shrubbery, and someone had just come up from behind us.

It was Benny's surveillance agent, who had been staking out the mine, hiding there all day, and watching.

They began speaking Hebrew and then Benny introduced him to us.

"Pappa, Koby, this is Shimon. He has been with me for a very long time. I saved his ass plenty of times and if it wasn't for me taking him under my wing, he would still be making bagels in Jerusalem!" Benny kidded.

"Shalom, nice to meet you," stated Shimon and he shook our hands with a firm right handed grip.

"Benny has told me about your time in the Holocaust. I am honored to meet you. And proud to fight with you!" he enthusiastically stated, and then he handed me his binoculars and I looked over the territory.

There were several barrack type buildings made of wood, and another small square building made of concrete block with its antiquated white paint peeling off of it, and it was heavily guarded.

"That's where they keep their jewels," Shimon stated.

The entrance into the mine was only a small opening about six foot wide and eight foot high, and it seemed all work had halted for the evening. It was quiet except for the sound of an enormous holding tank being filled up by a large fuel truck.

Not far from the mine was a large fancy villa, surrounded by exotic trees and lush gardens.

"That must be where those bastards are living," I said.

"I've seen enough. Let's go back," my father ordered.

As we walked back through the jungle, no one spoke.

I wondered if that was because we all were scared of the venomous snakes, or worried about our mission.

The longer we walked, the more I doubted our chances of capturing these two Nazi outlaws.

"I don't know, guys. Maybe we should rethink this, and bail out before we get into something we can't handle," I said.

"Same old Koby, Ticka, Ticka, Ticka!" jeered Benny.

"What are we going to do? Drive in with Kesh and shoot the place up?!" I exclaimed.

Benny immediately halted and hastily turned to me.

"YES!! You're exactly right! We are going to drive in and shoot up the place!

They think the only thing on our minds is buying Emeralds. But as soon as we get out of the car, they plan to restrain us, put us in cages, and torture us! They would probably let us heal up a bit and then start all over again! So the big surprise for them is going to be when we arrive, all hell is going to break loose, and we are going to fix those two pieces of shit along with all their Nazi scumbag guards!

Just turn on the "Ticker" in your head and you'll be fine!" exclaimed Benny.

I didn't say anymore. I probably shouldn't have ever told him about the ticking sound in my head when danger is present, and how it affects me, but he is my brother.

When we finally made it back to the farm house, it was late.

We tried to get some rest but the villa was so damn hot, it was impossible to get comfortable.

I laid on a bare mattress, once again thinking about our time on the run in Poland.

We were very lucky then... I pray our luck doesn't run out tomorrow.

Chapter 10

The following morning I awoke to the smell of eggs frying on the stove.

Sonya was preparing breakfast for us as my father and Benny were quietly whispering in the corner.

They stopped when they noticed me watching them.

My father walked over to me,

"There is going to be a change of plans," he stated.

"Oh that's good. I wasn't so keen on charging in and shooting up the place. What's the new plan?" I questioned.

"When Kesh shows up at the airport to pick us up tonight, Benny is going to attach a bomb underneath their car. They will quickly discover that we never arrived as planned. Thus, they will return to the mine empty handed," my father paused.

"We will be following them at a safe distance, as not to be seen. Heim's soldiers will surely be waiting for Kesh to return with us from the airport, and ready to ambush us. Once the driver enters the compound, they will surely encircle the car. However, they won't realize we are not in the car until it's too late. Shimon will detonate the car bomb, blowing them all back to hell.

After the bomb goes off, we'll crash through the gate with our truck and do our work.

If we can kill off the guards, Mengele and Heim will be easy to take. After all, they are not really soldiers. They're sniveling cowards, and most likely they will be hiding under their beds until the coast is clear!" my father stated.

"So what about Kesh? Do you plan to blow him up too?!" I exclaimed.

"Never mind him. He was the one who set this trap up for them. He'll get what he deserves!" Benny exclaimed.

"What if he didn't set it up and he is totally innocent? Are we now the judge, jury and executioner of all men...even men who are not Nazis?" I questioned.

My father turned to Benny;

"He's right," my father firmly commented.

I was shocked that my father actually agreed with me on something!

"Here's what we'll do," he continued.

"Sonya will disguise herself as an airport employee. She will find Kesh after he arrives in the airport and pass him a note attached to a baggage claim check.

It will read:

'Mr. Kesh, we could not find you, so we are taking a taxi to the mine. If you could pick up our delayed luggage I would appreciate it!

Mr. Joseph'

Then we'll see what he will do next. If he immediately runs to tip off the driver, Benny will be close by to hear what he has to say. Either he will be frantic that we threw a wrench in their scheme, or he will just do nothing, and go to the baggage claim where Benny will catch him and bring him back to us. The driver will ultimately return to the mine without Kesh, and we will continue on with the plan," stated my father.

"Sounds good to me," Benny replied.

"What if all this was not a trap at all? And there is no ambush. Maybe they really think we are coming to buy Emeralds?" I said.

"I don't know about that Koby. Things don't add up. Either way those Nazi 'murderers are gonna get what's coming to them. Short and Sharp!" replied Benny.

Just then Boris entered the house.

"Where were you?" my father questioned.

"I went to the outhouse. This isn't New York, you know!" proclaimed Boris.

"What time is Kesh supposed to pick us up tonight at the airport?" asked my father.

"Seven," I replied.

"Let's go over the plans and the layout of the mine a few more times," Benny proposed.

"Okay, we have the box truck with the cargo area covered with canvas. Boris you will be driving it, following the limo driver back to the mine. Shimon will be positioned in the hills overlooking the mine with the bomb detonator and his sniper rifle, and will be in contact with our radio. Sonya and I will be in the front with Boris. Papa and Koby you will be hidden in the back of the truck. When we arrive at the airport, I'll attach the bomb to the driver's car and then we'll wait to see how Kesh reacts. Either way we'll follow the driver back to the mine. When the gate opens to allow the returning car in, we'll wait for Shimon to detonate the bomb and we'll charge in right after it explodes. The rest we'll play by ear," Benny reiterated.

"What about Kesh?" I questioned.

If he is honest, he'll be in the back of the truck with you and Papa, but if he is working with Heim and Mengele, and setting us up in this ambush, he'll be in the car with Heims driver," replied Benny, and he ran his finger across his throat!

Shimon was ready. He left for his perch in the hills of the jungle, outside the perimeter of the mine.

He carried the car bomb detonator, a long rifle and a prayer book.

We were on edge all day long, and it seemed to take forever for night to come.

Most of the day we argued out of nervousness, but when we finally were ready to leave, we were united in spirit.

First we loaded up the truck with our guns and ammunition.

Benny mentioned he had almost forgotten something and went into the barn.

When he returned, he was carrying a long tubed instrument.

It was a shoulder launch bazooka!

"Just a little something extra that might come in handy," he stated.

"You don't happen to have a flamethrower in that barn, do you?" questioned my father.

Benny smiled and shook his head.

"No, I don't, but you probably wouldn't be able to light it up anyways, without me," Benny chuckled.

Before we left, we all sat down at Boris's kitchen table, and a prayer was said by my father;

"Bless us God, King of the Universe with strength and guidance. Shield us with thy powerful wings from this band of scourge so that we, your Chosen, who have journeyed so far to this desolate land to seek retribution. And to punish those who committed heinous atrocities against thy children. Energize us with thy power Lord, so that we may annihilate and destroy these wicked creatures who continue to slither on this Earth. Empower us Lord, bless our weapons with thy vengeance, and justice shall be served!..... Amen!"

Chapter 11

It was a somber moment, although I noticed that Boris wasn't really paying attention to my father's prayer. It was obvious that he had lost his faith in God. And considering what had happened to his family, who could blame him. We all then rose up from the table, and embraced each other, bidding one another a safe journey and victory. Before we marched out the door Benny shouted;

"Short and Sharp!" and it reaffirmed to us that we were the Chosen, and it charged us. And we left the Villa and entered the box truck.

Boris started the engine, ground up the gears with the stick shift and we drove off.

His driving was erratic, and we were tossed all around the back of the truck as he maneuvered the antiquated box truck through the winding and dilapidated roads of Sao Paulo.

"Boris, how did you ever get a driver's license!?" Benny exclaimed.

"It was easy, I gave the official two chickens and a bottle of schnapps and he gave me my license...why do you ask? You don't like how I drive?" Boris scorned.

"That explains it," stated Benny as he shook his head in disbelief.

We were getting close to the airport, and Benny was putting his finishing touches on the car bomb.

We cautiously entered the airport, and parked the truck in a loading zone in front of the Pan Am arrival's terminal.

Sonya, who had the prepared note, put on a black wig and an airport attendant's hat.

After approximately 30 minutes we noticed an old filthy black limousine that had pulled up to the sidewalk in front of us and parked.

We then saw Kesh quickly exit the limo and he ran into the terminal looking for us, while the driver remained outside and stayed in the car.

Boris pulled the truck right up behind the limo, almost crashing into its rear bumper, as Sonya exited the truck holding the note to give to Kesh.

Benny stealthily left the truck right behind her and crawled under the limousine from the rear as Sonia and our truck shielded him from view.

He quickly attached several large magnetic bundles of explosives to the underside of the car, and then he casually crawled out, brushed himself off and followed Sonya into the terminal.

He sat on a bench pretending to read a newspaper, while he secretly observed Kesh.

We received a radio call from Shimon, stating that there was activity at the mine.

The guards were armed and positioning themselves all around the premises!

However, there was no sighting of Heim and Mengele, he reported.

"No Heim and Mengele? They might be gone!" I cried.

"Those schmucks will most likely stay in the villa until their guards have captured us. Don't forget these two scumbags are not fighters. They will let others risk their necks to do their dirty work," stated my father.

Boris reversed the truck back to the loading area, when we noticed Sonya quickly leaving the terminal.

Boris flashed the truck's lights and she ran towards us and jumped into the front seat.

"How did it go, did he recognize you?" my father asked through the opening in the back of the truck's cab.

"When I tapped him on the shoulder, he grabbed his jacket and closed it tightly crossing his arms across his chest! He was extremely jumpy! I think he thought I was going to steal his precious diamond vest! I handed him the note and walked away," Sonya stated.

We watched the airport doors intently, waiting to see if Kesh was going to return to the limousine.

Suddenly we heard a tumult behind the truck. The canvas canopy doors flung open and Kesh was propelled into the back of the truck with us.

"Mr. Kesh! Nice of you to drop in!" I said in relief.

"Nice to see you too, Mr. Jacob, Mr. Joseph, and Mr. Benny!" Kesh replied.

"That was Sonya who gave you the note," said Benny.

"Listen, someting has gone wrong at da mine! I overheard dem talking about killing you for what you did in da war. Dey said you poisoned Albert's father in a bar in Stockholm," Kesh reported.

"What luck! One of those bastards who drank that rat poison was Adolf Heim! Albert's Uncle!" Benny exclaimed.

"Yes, Mr. Benny. Dey knew you were in New York. A spy saw me going into your store. I didn't know anything, but dey sent me invitations for years to come buy Emeralds from dem. Dey begged me to bring da Jew Watchmaker to buy goods from dem, and dey promised me dey would give me a percentage of da sale. But I never wanted to bring anyone to my sources. Da percentage wasn't worth da money dat I could resell the goods for," Kesh stated.

"That sounds exactly like you, Kesh," I declared.

Kesh went on;

"Da driver had a gun and told me dat I better not say anything to you or an assassin stationed inside da airport would kill all of us. When Sonya tapped me on da shoulder, I thought it was him!

How did you become aware of dis mine? I have a feeling you are not really interested in buying Emeralds," Kesh exclaimed.

"Heim and Mengele are notorious Nazi war criminals on the run. They are wanted by Germany, the USA and Israel for crimes against humanity.

Boris has a personal interest, and asked us to help take them down," I explained.

Just then Boris tapped on the metal ceiling above his seat.

"The driver has gotten out of the car and is looking for Mr. Kesh!" Boris stated.

"Okay, It's 'Showtime!' Everyone get ready!" Benny commanded.

Sonya changed into a black combat jump suit equipped with two Hari Kari knives, one on her leg and the other on her back. She had several razor-sharp Shuriken throwing stars and a long sheathed Samurai sword attached to a black braided silk Ninja belt. A leg holster was tightly strapped to her leg equipped with an Uzi submachine gun and across her chest a bandolier of ammunition clips.

"What do you need the gun for?" I sarcastically questioned.

Benny was also changing into a similar outfit. He had the same weapons as Sonya, except he wore his father's Chalaf over his shoulder on his back.

"Where's my jumpsuit?" I complained in jest.

My father and I checked our machine guns and strapped on our ammunition belts.

Benny and Sonya left the back of the truck and got into the front, while Boris continued observing the limo from the driver's seat.

He suddenly reported that the limo driver had just returned and was frantically searching for Kesh, and he jumped back into his car and was speeding away.

"Let's go! If he stops to call anyone, kill him!" Benny ordered.

"What's happening at the mine?" my father asked.

Benny radioed Shimon but there was no response.

"Shit!! They have Shimon!" he exclaimed.

"How do you know that?" my father questioned.

"If he does not respond, he is either dead or captured!"

"Now how will we detonate the car bomb?!" I shouted.

"Koby, you worry too much!" replied Benny and he removed a second detonator switch from the glove compartment.

"Like Noah's ark, we do everything in two's," Sonia stated.

Chapter 12

The limousine driver was speeding and driving erratically on his way back to the mine.

We followed with our lights off as not to be seen, but fortunately we had a near full moon and thus had some visibility.

As we bounced around in the back of the truck, it reminded me of the ride in the back of the German staff car, when we were dressed as Nazis heading to Treblinka, searching for my Mother and Hanna.

Benny and I had been sitting in the back seat, and it was my father doing the reckless driving.

Suddenly an ominous gut wrenching feeling came over me, one I had suppressed for many years.

I hadn't felt it since we left Sweden, over ten years ago.

I could hear the distinct ticking of my father's wristwatch, and I drifted back to the first time I remembered hearing his watch ticking, it was when we were in the basement of our watch shop, and hiding in our secret room from the Nazis.

Then suddenly Benny began barking orders and my silent daydream was shattered.

"Koby and Papa, you will make your way to the villa while Sonia and I eliminate the guards. Heim and Mengele will probably be watching from their cozy home until they are sure we are captured!" Benny ordered.

"What's going on here, Mr. Joseph?!" Kesh exclaimed.

"We're on a mission, and you have just become a part of it!" my father stated.

"Wait a minute. I just want to sit dis ting out. Can't you drop me off at a bus stop or someting?" he nervously questioned.

"Sorry, Kesh, you'll have to come with us," I replied.

Clearly he was petrified, and as he was being tossed about on the floor of the truck, he clutched onto his precious gemstones in his vest, and began reciting his prayers in Hindi.

"Okay, we are getting close to the gates of the mine!" Boris shouted.

We slowed down as we watched the mine's iron gate swing open to allow the limousine into the compound and then it quickly closed. The driver was honking his horn to alert the guards that something was wrong and not to start shooting.

Again I heard my father's watch ticking, and I started to go numb as the sound intensified.

"Tick, Tick, Tick, Tick."

Once again after all these years, it drummed into my skull! I could see Benny through the empty window opening into the passenger compartment of the truck, staring intently into the compound as he held his thumb on the car bomb's detonator.

He was talking loudly but everything was silent to me except the "Ticking" sound that echoed in my brain!

The limo quickly drove in and abruptly stopped in the middle of the compound.

A group of approximately forty guards rushed towards the car with their guns drawn, shouting at the presumed occupants to get out with their hands up!

When the driver opened the door, Benny pushed the button on the detonator!

The car instantly exploded into a fierce fireball, blowing up everyone who was around it! Bodies went flying through the air in all directions as the smoke from the blast filled the compound!

"Go Boris!!" shouted Benny.

Suddenly my brain went into shock. Everything slowed down including the ticking,... ticking,........ ticking.

Boris accelerated, and the truck rammed through the iron gates and barreled into the compound!

The Guards that were up in the Watchtower began opening fire on us!!

Then more Nazi guards came rushing out from everywhere as Benny and Sonya vaulted out of the truck as it was still moving!

They seemed to tumble in some sort of Ninja assassin acrobatic maneuver as they hit the ground!

Meanwhile my father and I began emptying our bullet clips at the watchtower guards, as Benny and Sonya fought their way toward the mine.

The ticking I had almost forgotten had returned to my brain!

As our lives were threatened, time began to slow down.

I watched in slow motion as Benny and Sonya raced fearlessly toward the guards, their faces filled with rage and retribution.

They both were astounding as they fearlessly fought with their spectacular martial arts hand-to-hand combat skills!

Time seemed virtually to stand still as I watched Sonya and Benny viciously fight, swirling their Samurai swords, and slaughtering the Nazi guards, slicing and chopping them to pieces as they dodged their oncoming bullets!

They spun, tumbled and flipped as they flailed their razor sharp swords like fan blades in the wind, working in tandem, as they were both ferociously desecrating the sinister guards!

They were a methodical killing machine, as Benny would slice their bodies, Sonia would finish them off with a decapitating stroke or a stab to the heart! Their vile black blood gushed and splattered everywhere as the Nazi guards were slaughtered by the savage duo!

My father and I continued firing our Uzi's on the countless guards that were pouring out from everywhere, until it seemed that there were none left standing on their feet.

The smoke from the car bomb was dissipating, and I instantly noticed Kesh scurrying out of the truck, and entering the white cement block building where they stored the mined Emeralds.

"Typical Kesh...risking his life to loot some gems!" I thought.

At this point there were now scores of disfigured bodies laying   motionless in pools of ungodly black hearted blood.

Benny and Sonya had single handedly killed off most of the guards, and they made their way back toward us, drenched in splattered blood. It was incredible to witness what they had done, and the manner in which they had done it!

"We have to get to the villa before Heim and Mengele get away!" Benny shouted.

As we raced towards it, gunfire from the villa began pouring out.

A German with a mauser machine gun was perched up on the villa's roof.

We were pinned down behind the giant rock crusher!

"What are we going to do now?!" I shouted.

Just then we heard the rev of the truck's engine. Boris sped by us and crashed the vehicle into the side of the villa!

We quickly moved forward and began shooting at the points of entry.

When we passed the truck, I noticed Boris was slouched over and unconscious behind the steering wheel.

The machine gunner was jarred by the impact, and he fell off the roof. He was hanging by one arm onto the rain gutter and dangling in the air.

Sonya instantly removed a serrated throwing star from her belt and whipped it through the air, striking and completely lacerating the Nazi's throat, and he morbidly screamed as he came crashing to the ground!

My father and I circled around to the back of the house, where we were able to finish off the remaining resistance.

Then the area suddenly became totally silent.

Benny and Sonya then charged toward the front door in tandem, and with a flying leap, they broke it from its hinges with their feet and it went crashing inward and onto the floor.

They stood in the doorway breathing heavily, with their bloody swords in hand, poised in a ninja warrior stance, as my father and I charged in right behind them!

Chapter 13

We stormed into the villa and to our amazement, a glass wall divided and separated the room we were in.

Behind the glass was a dark spherical metal and glass chamber, and inside we could see the silhouette of three small figures.

Next to the chamber was Heim's diabolical laboratory.

In the darkness we could barely make out the two upright male figures watching us from behind the glass, and another person who was shackled to an electrocution-style chair with a sack over his head.

In front of the glass wall, was a large bronze bust of Adolf Hitler perched on a small round table, along with three large steins of beer that were carefully placed on petite swastika coasters.

The laboratory was deliberately decorated with countless German and Nazi flags, along with other Nazi regalia.

This place was Heim's sadistic laboratory.

It was filled with all sorts of chemicals, scientific equipment and the barbaric tools Heim would use to torture his victims.

From behind the protective glass wall, a light switched on and two men dressed in finely pressed Nazi SS uniforms revealed themselves.

It was none other than Josef Mengele and Albert Heim!

Despite the fact that each and every one of their guards were dead, they seemed confident and in control.

My father wasted no time and opened fire, trying to shatter the glass!

But the glass was bulletproof and the bullets failed to penetrate it.

"Shit!!" my father whispered to me.

"Well done, Juden! We've been expecting you!" jeered Heim, and then both Heim and Mengele exuberantly applauded.

"The way I see it, we have you two cockroaches outnumbered and in an unfortunate predicament, Heim. You're trapped in your aquarium, and maybe we'll just light a fire and burn you two to a crisp, just as you two have done with the innocent bodies of so many that you murdered," my father replied.

"Ahh yes, that would be unfortunate for us. However, as you can see, we have four prisoners, three of which are restrained in our 'Final solution parlor'. My, doesn't that sound inviting? It sounds so much more appealing than the harsh 'gas chamber' we used to refer to it as in the old days, wouldn't you agree, Watchmaker? But sadly, if you burn down my luxurious villa, you will certainly also kill these 3 innocent bystanders, and your filthy Mossad agent," stated Heim.

Benny suddenly began shouting out in Hebrew to Shimon, who was shackled in the chair.

"Shut up your Jew speak!!" Heim shouted.

Shimon replied that they had ambushed him and taken him prisoner!

"Who are those other people in the chamber?!" demanded my father.

"We have time for that, Watchmaker. Let's just chat a bit first," Heim cordially stated.

"Bitte, where are our manners, cousin? Watchmaker, first and foremost, Dr. Mengele and I would both like to welcome you all to our humble villa. Please accept our generous hospitality, but unfortunately you will only be our guests for a short time, and then very shortly you will be suffering an egregiously slow death, so please don't get too comfortable. You all must be very thirsty after all that fighting. Would you all like to enjoy a nice cold beer?" Heim maniacally stated, and he used his hands to display the fact that there were three full steins of beer which were placed on the table before us.

"No thank you. We are not very thirsty. But why don't you and your little monkey come out from behind your pet shop window so we can speak man to monkey?" jeered my father.

"Very funny, Watchmaker. But we will soon see how funny you really are!" Heim sneered.

Benny and Sonya scanned the room, searching for any signs of weakness.

I stood close to my father and noticed that the "Ticking" sound which had been drumming in my head, had dissipated and was now gone.

Despite the barrier of the bulletproof glass, we still kept our guns trained on the two men, although in a more relaxed manner.

"What's the matter with you, Mengele? Can't you talk? Or did torturing all those poor innocent children turn you into a moronic inbred stooge?" my father taunted.

We all laughed hysterically, heckling him which was causing Mengele to become frustrated.

"Shut, shut up your mouths, you stupid Jews!" he stammered as he tried to save face.

"You know Mengele, there is a big scary man outside with a nasty scar on the back of his head, a scar which you were responsible for. After all these years, he has been anxiously awaiting to meet you again, his name is Boris Wilensky. I'm sure you will remember him when he greets you. Your henchmen tore his two little boys from his desperate hold on them, and then you butchered his two little boys in Auschwitz for sport. As you can probably imagine he is fairly upset, and he would like to have a little conversation with you about what you did to his precious little boys. Maybe this time you will hear him, unlike the way you mocked and rudely ridiculed him at Auschwitz. But, I can assure you, that this time you are going to hear this man speak very loudly and clearly tonight, and you are going to pay dearly for what you did to his two little boys, and for everyone else who were your guests, for that matter?" taunted my father.

A panicked look came over Mengele, and he began nervously speaking German to Heim.

Heim tried to calm him down, and told him he had everything under control.

"Watchmaker, do you know why I lured you here, to my Emerald mine?" Heim questioned.

Benny raised his hand as a schoolboy would who knew the right answer!

"I know, I know! Is it because I spiked your Nazi pervert father beer with rat poison in Stockholm! Do I win a prize now?!" Benny cheered.

"Shut up, Swinehunt!" shouted Heim.

"Actually, Heim, you didn't lure us here at all. We came looking for Mengele, but it will be our pleasure to eradicate you as well," stated my father.

"You seem confident you will succeed despite your compromised position," Heim sneered.

"Papa, do you know which of those Nazi lunatics was Albert's cowardly father? Was he the one who was beating himself senseless over the head with the broken table leg, or was he the one who was banging his head against the bar until his head split open and his green brains burst out all over the floor?!" heckled Benny.

"I'm not sure which one he was, but they all got what they deserved! It was grotesque and revolting, though. The way they manically thrashed about, puking beer and all the blood squirting out of their eyeballs. Yuck, it really almost made me vomit too! But I considered what filthy scourge they were, and it was then more satisfying watching them flailing about, all over the bar room, self mutilating and beating themselves senseless! So which one of those unlucky swine was your papa, Heim?" matter-of-factly stated by my father.

"We'll see how funny you are when I show you who I have in this chamber!" threatened Heim.

He pushed a button and the chamber illuminated.

We were shocked and horrified to see that it was Hanna, and Benny's two little girls imprisoned in the chamber! They were strapped into chairs with blindfolds covering their eyes!

"Not so funny now, are you, Watchmaker?" laughed Heim, and Mengele also joined in.

"As you all know I have a fondness for children. I can't wait to dissect them!" Mengele salivated.

My father stood there poised and rubbing his chin. Benny and Sonya desperately tried to restrain their emotions.

"Isn't it amazing, Watchmaker, how we were able to kidnap your children right out from under your big Jew noses! German ingenuity will always prevail!" exclaimed Heim.

"What are you talking about, Albert? That's not my daughter," my father firmly stated.

"And those aren't my kids, either," Benny joined in.

"Of course those are your daughters!" shouted Heim.

"I'm telling you, Albert, I should know what my own daughter looks like. You Dummkopfs made a mistake!" exclaimed my father.

Mengele became nervous again, and the two men began arguing in their German tongue.

"Good try, Watchmaker! The table in front of you with the three beer steins, they are full of Germany's finest brew, and an extra special ingredient that I'm sure you won't enjoy," laughed Heim.

"Actually, Albert, we prefer American beer. Do you have any ice cold Budweiser draught? And unfortunately, you are one stein short. I believe my daughter-in-law is thirsty too!" my father jeered.

Heim became frustrated and picked up a Nazi emblemed hourglass!

"You see this hourglass. It was a gift to me from Hitler himself, for killing so many of you Jews! When I tip this glass over, you will then have ten minutes to drink those beers! If you refuse I will engage the gas capsules in the chamber and your children will die before your eyes!" Heim decreed.

"What kind of scheist German hourglass is that? Isn't it supposed to last an hour...not just ten minutes? Let's use my watch instead, since I know it's more accurate than that half assed Hitler hour glass of yours," my father proclaimed.

Heim ground his teeth in frustration and shouted,

"Drink the beer or watch your children die!!"

My father calmly stood there and replied;

"Go ahead Albert, pull the lever now, because as I told you, that girl in there is not my daughter and I can prove it! For all I know those could be your Nazi inbred mongaloid kids in there, and the chamber is fake! But just one more thing Heim; you pull that lever and we'll burn down the house with you and your monkey in it!"

Mengele became nervously agitated, and then he confronted Albert!

"You were the one who convinced me to help you kill these Jews. But your idiot men abducted the wrong offspring, Sheist kopf! And now we are trapped in a compromised situation!

You said the Watchmaker and his boys would drink the poison to save their children, and that we would just walk out of here!" ranted Mengele.

"Calm down. You keep forgetting we are officers of the Third Reich! Keep your cool, Josef," exclaimed Heim.

He thought for a moment and then spoke again, addressing my father.

"Watchmaker, you said you can prove that this girl is not your daughter. Enlighten me." said Heim.

"It's simple," my father declared.

"Just remove her blindfold and you will see this child will not recognize me."

"And if she does recognize you, you will agree to drink the beer. Your word, Watchmaker?" stated Heim.

"Agreed. And you let them go after we are dead, they are innocent. But if she doesn't know me, you let them go, and we kill you and Joseph. Agreed, Albert?" matter-of-factly replied my father.

"Agreed," Heim sarcastically responded.

We all knew that Heim would never honor his end of the bargain, no matter what the outcome was. But neither would we, however it was buying us some needed time.

Heim whispered to Mengele and then directed him to open the chamber and remove Hanna's blindfold.

As he lifted the blindfold, Hanna appeared dazed and expressionless.

It was just as she had been years before, when we found her on the death march.

"See Albert, I told you she was not my daughter. Now you can let them go!" exclaimed my father.

Heim laughed as my father approached the glass wall.

"You must be really stupid, Watchmaker! To believe I would let anyone out of here alive!" Heim exclaimed.

My father raised his hand and made a fist as he approached the glass wall.

The Nazis grinned as they believed he was going to drink the beer, but instead he firmly pressed the large red diamond that was mounted in his ring against the glass wall and scored a giant hooplike circle into the glass.

"You can't cut a hole in this glass with a ruby!" Heim laughed.

My father then sternly reached down to the table which supported the three steins of poisonous beer and the bust of Hitler, as if he was going to lift two glasses of the beer, but instead he took hold of Hitler's bust.

With both hands he heaved up the heavy bronze effigy over his head, and smashed it against the score he had etched into the glass wall! The glass wavered and flexed for a moment, and then everything went completely silent.

Chapter 14

We all froze, as we held our breaths and stared at the deeply scored scratch in the glass wall.

Heim and Mengele began laughing at my father's failed attempt to break the glass, but then after a second or two, the score began to crackle and formed a deep visible crack where my father had traced it! When my father began striking the wall over and over again with the bust, the crack began to travel and it raced all the way around the exact path of the score in a complete circle!

At that moment, Benny and Sonya leapt through the air and kicked the glass circle!

The round section instantly broke free, and it crashed onto the floor inside Heim's lab!

Suddenly we were face to face with those two demonic creatures!

Benny and Sonya instantly jumped through the giant hole, and my father and I followed!

Heim tried to activate the gas chamber's Zyklon B gas pellets, but Sonya cartwheeled through the air, and wrenched his neck between her two legs, and slammed him violently backwards onto the floor.

Benny smashed in Mengele's nose with a head butt to the face causing him to collapse, and he huddled on the floor in a fetal position, weeping, while blood gushed from his mutilated nose.

I placed my foot on his neck and my gun barrel into his ear, as Benny and my father raced into the gas chamber and released the children.

"We're home free! We did it!" I thought.

But then suddenly I heard a rip of machine gun fire coming from behind us!

Shimon was instantly shot dead in his restraints, and my father and Benny jumped out of the chamber, but it was too late!

"Drop your weapons!!" a familiar voice ordered.

Sonya had no choice but to release her constricting hold of her locked legs from Heim's neck.

He slowly got up and brushed himself off.

"Excellent work, Herr Kesh!!" Heim jubilantly complimented.

Kesh smugly stood there, maniacally chuckling.

"You're very welcome, Herr partner," he replied back to Heim.

"Now, all of you, get into the gas chamber!" Heim sternly ordered.

Mengele sprang to his feet while agonizingly holding his bloody nose, but Benny was able to give him a solid knee to the groin on his way up. He buckled over and collapsed to the floor again, rolling and moaning from the excruciating pain!

"Ouch Mengele, that must have hurt!" Benny taunted.

My father turned to Kesh, as he stood on the opposite side of the opening of the glass wall, and was pointing a German submachine gun at us.

"You know, Mr. Kesh...or shall I call you Herr Kesh, you really had me fooled. I thought you were an honorable man. But now I see you are a piece of shit just like your friends here," stated my father.

"Just business, Mr. Joseph. Dey paid me a lot of money to get you here. So why don't you just go over and get into dat gas ball and let dem kill you, so I can go home, Sir. And by da way, Mr. Joseph. Could you hand me over dat Red Diamond ring from your finger, der is a gentleman in New York who is very interested in it?" Kesh stated.

"You would let these monsters kill these three innocent little girls and us, for the money? exclaimed my father.

"Well it's not just for da money, Mr. Joseph. Dere are also da Emeralds, too!" Kesh greedily replied.

"You can have the diamond when I'm dead, Kesh," my father boldly stated.

Kesh smiled, and nodded his head in gleeful anticipation as he kept his gun trained on us.

"Now, get into the chamber!" shouted Heim.

We slowly walked toward the metal entrance door of the gas chamber.

The "Ticking" in my brain began to echo, as we each stepped in.

First Sonya, then Benny, then my father.

"You get in der too, Mr. Jacob!" Kesh calmly shouted.

Everyone was quiet as Benny and Sonya hugged their children and my father held Hanna.

"So, I suppose these actually were your children, Watchmaker? I must say, it's odd only killing so few Jews in our gas chamber. In the good old days we were able to gas hundreds of your filthy kind at a time," sneered Heim.

The "Ticking" in my brain began decelerating as we all were facing certain death. My heart pounded as I entered the chamber and my state of mind once again drifted into a state of surrealness and slow motion. It was finally over for all of us, we lost everything over this mission of retribution. But we believed we were the Chosen ones to eradicate these evil monsters, and so it had to be done. Whatever happens to us now, I presume it will be God's will.

Giddily, Mengele began pushing the heavy metal door closed behind me, as we were all crammed into the compact gas chamber.

Kesh smiled, and sarcastically waved "Bye-Bye" to us, and we heard them all manically laughing through the dense metal and glass walls of the gas chamber.

"Where is my grandfather's shooting star now?" I thought.

"Tick... tick,....tic.

Chapter 15

I instantly noticed the sour smell of the poisonous gas pellets as I wrapped my arms around my entire family, and told them I loved them all.

My father and Benny began reciting the mourner's prayer in Hebrew, as I stood silent, hoping to be reunited with my mother and grandparents once again.

"Tick, tick, tick…" hammered in my brain as all was lost.

The two Nazi's now believed that they were back in control and triumphant. Mengele gleefully began pushing the chamber door closed, and he laughed uncontrollably! I noticed Heim rejoicing as I peered through one of the gas chambers' tiny observation windows, as he took hold of the red lever, which would activate the Zyklon B gas pellets.

Then suddenly at that instant, I heard a loud screaming, whistling noise rapidly approaching toward us, and the villa began to vibrate!

At first I thought it was the sound of the gas pellets dissolving in the acid! But then I quickly noticed that Heims attention was now directed towards Kesh, and he had quickly moved away from the release lever, and was now holding up his hands in front of his face in a horrified manner! Kesh's body suddenly exploded and he was obliterated and blown to pieces! His rancid guts and appendages violently splattered in all directions along with his hundreds of packets of Emeralds and other gems that were concealed in his precious vest! Everyone was thrown back from the force of the blast as a projectile unleashed its fury on Heims sadistic Laboratory! Amazingly, the iron chamber actually protected us from the explosion and we were unharmed!

When the smoke quickly dissipated, we noticed Boris sternly standing in the doorway, and he dropped the shoulder held bazooka on to the floor!

Heim and Mengele were coughing and stumbling around the smokey laboratory as we jubilantly dashed out of the chamber!

Benny and I restrained the two Nazi doctors, while my father released the children and sent them outside with Sonya.

Benny gripped Heim from behind with his arm around his throat. My father then tore off Heim's Nazi jacket and shirt, revealing the black swastika tattoo below his armpit.

Boris's face raged with madness as he rushed in and seized Mengele away from me!

Finally, he was able to get his hands on this demonic tyrant who murdered his two little boys.

He bore his sharp fingernails into Mengele's throat as he emphatically clutched him from behind, and clenched his deathly black hair with his other hand, forcing Mengele to watch and witness the fate of his cousin!

I used a piece of wire to bind Mengele's arms behind his back as Boris repeatedly whispered his family's names over and over into Mengele's ear, as he tightly clung onto that vile demon.

"Sarah, Katriel, Jenya!... Sarah, Katriel, Jenya!... Sarah, Katriel, Jenya!!" over and over again, he assertively whispered their names and dug his long sharp fingernails deeper into Mengele's throat!

"Albert Heim, you murdered countless innocent men, women and children for this ugly swastika!" Benny proclaimed as he pointed at Heims swastika which was tattooed under his armpit.

Benny then reached over his shoulder and slowly drew his father's sacred Chalaf from its sheath, and began carving off the skin and flesh that bore that ugly hideous symbol of hate.

Heim screamed in bitter agony as Benny sliced through his bloody flesh, and balanced it on his blade, for all to see.

Benny then tossed me the hunk of bloody meat from his blade, and I began forcing it into Heim's mouth, as he vehemently resisted.

"How does shit taste, Doctor?!" I shouted.

Meanwhile, my father released Shimon's dead body from the chair and carefully placed him on the floor.

"Put Heim in his chair!" my father ordered.

Benny and I forced Heim into it, as he desperately resisted and struggled.

We tightly strapped his arms, legs and torso onto the large frame of the hideous, sadistic chair.

My father reached into one of the drawers in Heim's laboratory and removed a large bottle of acid.

"I think this might hurt a bit," my father stated.

And he began pouring the acid all over Heims constrained hands. Heim screamed at the top of his lungs, as the acid fizzed and smoked as it melted away his skin!

"How many Christians, Jews and other innocent victims did you torture and kill?! Who were the lost souls that you carved up for fun with those murderous hands, Albert?!! How many children did you murder and desecrate, Albert?!!! Tell me how could you sleep at night after hearing the screams of your victims as they were never anesthetized and then butchered by you, Albert?!!!!" my father passionately interrogated.

Even in his dire agony the perverted doctor was able to respond,

"I slept like a Jew baby, just like the ones I carved up for my Christmas dinner!" jeered Heim.

Benny viciously swung his Chalaf and instantly shaved off one of Heim's ears!

He screamed as blood was gushing from the side of his head.

I picked up a piece of burning shrapnel with a pair of pliers and pressed the red hot metal against his bleeding wound, searing it to a crisp.

He continued to shriek in agony as his flesh sizzled and burned.

Meanwhile Mengele was having a mental breakdown as he was forced to witness what his dear cousin was enduring.

He begged Boris to let him go and kept frantically repeating,

"I was just following orders! I was just following orders!" Boris abruptly turned Mengele around to face him!

"Do you recognize me, Mengele?!!" Boris shouted.

"Maybe you will remember me by the scars on my wrist caused by my clenched fingernails, as I fought to hold onto my boys as your Nazi dogs tore them from me! Maybe you will remember me better by my two little boys who you butchered and carved out their eyes and teeth before you murdered them. Maybe you will remember me by the way, I picked them up from the pile of dozens of dead children in your laboratory, and how I carried them back to the ovens as you laughed! Do you recognize me now, Mengele?!!" Boris roared.

With his bare hand Boris tightened his grip and sunk his sharp fingernails into Mengele's throat, and began ripping the skin away from his neck exposing his veins and windpipe.

"This is how hard I held onto my children when you had them torn away from me!" Boris shouted.

Mengele's screams and shrieks were deafening!

My father shouted to Boris to take him outside and kill him.

Boris dragged him out of the villa by his long black hair, as the beast struggled and twisted, desperately trying to escape.

Benny searched the lab and found the large bottle of the rat poison, a portion of which Heim had poured into the beers.

My father gathered up a length of thin rubber surgical hose and forced it up Heim's nose, and continued pushing it all the way up into his nasal cavity, and it continued all the way down the back of his throat, and into his stomach.

Then he methodically connected the other end of the hose to the large brown glass bottle of rat poison with a rubber cork, which had a hose connector passing through it.

"We are going to do an experiment with you Albert, if you don't mind. We all know how much you enjoy good old Nazi research," my father sarcastically stated and then he noticed the filthy and battered Nazi hourglass in a pile of rubble on the floor, and he picked it up.

"Albert, if you are still alive when the sand runs out of this glass, we will spare you the horrific death by poisoning and just shoot you in the head. Otherwise you are going to die a grueling slow death like your swine faced father," my father jeered.

"Here, pinch this hose tightly between what's left of your burned emaciated fingers, Albert. But please, try not to let it go, or sadly the poison will drip through the hose and go directly into your stomach!" my father warned.

"Ten minutes is not such a long time, Albert! Come on! you can do it! You've gutted babies in less time than that!" Benny exclaimed, as he sarcastically cheered him on.

My father placed the soft rubber tube between Heim's grotesquely mutilated fingers, and raised the bottle and hung it with a piece of wire from an overhead light fixture hanging down from the ceiling.

At first, Heim clenched it tightly with his disfigured fingers, not allowing any of the fluid to flow through.

"Albert Heim, you are hereby notified that you are here before us and placed on trial for crimes against humanity. For killing, torturing and showing no mercy or compassion to thousands of innocent human victims!

How do you plead, Heim?" questioned my father.

"Kiss my ass!" Heim moaned.

"Very well! We the jury unanimously find you guilty as charged, and sentence you to rot in the tar pits of hell, you vile demon!" my father commanded.

He then picked up a large bottle of acetone from a cabinet of chemicals, and he drenched the flammable liquid all over Heim's legs!

"This is for the victims you sent to the ovens, Albert Heim!" my father stated.

And he lit a match and threw it onto Heim's lap, and his pants instantly burst into a flaming inferno!

Heim screamed at the top of his lungs as the fire furiously blazed all over his legs, and it quickly began to burn away through the fabric of his gestapo pants!

The odor of burning meat filled the room.

It was a familiar smell that we recognized when we had passed by Treblinka.

"Albert, do you have any marshmallows around here!" Benny joked.

"Relax, Albert, once the acetone burns up the fire will go out," I stated.

The fire quickly subsided as Heim continued screaming and shrieking.

Through this, he remarkably continued to firmly hold the hose between his disintegrating fingers.

His legs and abdomen were now grotesquely burned and blistered, and the smoke drifted upward toward the ceiling.

I removed the Japanese Hari Kari knife from Benny's sheath, and stood in front of Heim as he continued to keep his grip on the hose. I glanced over at the hour glass and noticed that the sand was halfway gone.

"I see that the hour glass is half empty, Albert. " I reluctantly stated.

Benny interjected;

"Actually brother, I was going to say it was half full. You're such a pessimist!" he sarcastically stated.

I shook my head and continued;

"I understood that you preferred experimenting on your victims while they were awake, with no anesthesia, Dr. Heim. You enjoyed cutting them up into pieces while you entertained yourself. Can you imagine how painful that must have been?" Heim was silent as he struggled to hold his grip on the hose.

"No? You can't? I can demonstrate to you how it must have felt?" I affirmed.

I took the large knife and began carving a large thick swastika into his chest.

He clenched his teeth, refusing to show any sign of pain.

It was surprising that he was still able to hold back the flow of the poison for so long, as I continued pressing the knife's point deeply into his skin!

As I bore down, his grip on the rubber hose began to soften.

First a few drops of poison trickled down through the tube.

Then a few more, until he could no longer hold it back.

The bottle quickly bubbled and emptied in a matter of seconds.

Some air bubbles finally raced back up through the tube, and then all of the poison was gone from the bottle.

He sat there quietly with a grin on his face, as if he was expecting nothing to happen and that he would be okay.

After a minute, Heim began to thrash about and had freakish jerking convulsions.

Benny glanced over at the hour glass, and saw that time had just run out.

"I guess you didn't make it, Albert. Give my regards to your father when you meet him in hell!" Benny exclaimed.

"Come, let's go outside. We don't need to see this," my father suggested.

As we passed by, each of us spat on his face, and I poured the remaining acetone all around the laboratory and threw a match on it as we prepared to leave the villa.

We quickly wrapped Shimon's body in a sheet and then the three of us carefully carried him outside, and placed him in the passenger seat of the truck, concealing his body from the children.

Chapter 16

In the distance, I heard a loud burst of thunder and I gazed up at the sky. Humongous black and grey ominous clouds were gathering and were quickly rolling in.

There were bellowing violent thunder claps and massive lightning strikes all around us! The treacherous clouds were increasing in size and volume as a massive storm was bearing down upon us!

The extreme winds fanned the flames of the burning villa and it became consumed in a massive blazing fire.

After we left the building, we could hear Heim screaming and shrieking in agony, but the blazing timber and high winds began to quickly drown out his horrific clamor!

"Justice has been served!" shouted my father as the strong winds blew harder, and a lightning bolt had just struck and split a nearby tree.

"Yes, Papa, he got what he deserved!" I shouted back.

My father moved the truck from the burning villa and we watched as Boris dragged Mengele to the rock crusher. Sonya then helped the children and Hanna into the back of the truck. She told them not to look as she tried to shield their view.

Dead bodies were everywhere, and Benny hurdled over them as he raced over to assist Boris secure Mengele down to the rock crushers conveyor belt.

The winds continued to rage violently as Benny struggled to reach Boris!

Boris recklessly picked up Mengele and forcefully threw him down onto the rock crushers conveyor belt, with his feet pointing inward, towards the mouth of the giant machine.

Enraged by what this beast had done to his children, Boris held him down by clenching him by his mutilated bleeding throat with his thick brawny hand. And then, with his powerful fingers and his razor sharp fingernails, he gouged his fingers deeply down through the naked flesh and exposed arteries of his throat, and clawed his way through the dense muscle and tendon surrounding Mengele's windpipe! Then Boris squeezed with all his might, strangling the evil demon as he began vehemently pounding Mengele's face with his other fist! Benny had just showed up, and only then Boris released Mengele from his deathly grip.

"You are not going to die so fast, Mengele!" Boris raged.

Huge lightning bolts were striking all around us, and the loud crackling thunder that immediately followed was so powerful it shook the earth!

The storm raged over the mine, and I thought to myself that this was not like any other storm that I had ever seen before.

There was no rain, and strangely, the storm appeared to be isolated only over the mining compound!

Mengele continued shrieking and begging to be let go.

"I was following orders!" he dismally shouted over and over.

Benny took hold of him by his jet-black hair, and pulled his face closer to his, and then stared deeply into Mengele's black satanic eyes.

"I am sick of listening to you and your lying Nazi scum making the excuse that you were following orders!

Nazi shit like you murdered my mother and father! Were they all just following orders! Not one of you murderous letches ever showed a bit of empathy or compassion to anyone!" Benny shouted.

He then ceremoniously reached over his shoulder and drew out his father's Chalaf from its protective sheath.

"Mengele! This was my father's Sheckets blade as was his father's blade before him. Now this blade is mine to seek retribution and pass judgement on you merciless Nazi bastards! My father once gave me an order before he was killed by your Nazi swine..."Short and Sharp!" Benny shouted.

He then raised the butt of the knife and hammered it down into Mengele's mouth, shattering his gaping front teeth! He then began prying his mouth open with the knife's handle, and he took hold of Mengele's slithering tongue! He began pulling and stretching it out of his bloody mouth as Mengele resisted and squirmed about!

Meanwhile, Boris turned the key and started the rock crusher's giant diesel engine.

Its massive iron hammers slowly began churning up and down, until they built up speed and achieved a loud powerful banging rhythm.

The conveyor belt was governed by a long metal lever, which allowed its operator to control the belt.

Boris watched as Benny twirled his blade around his hand in some form of martial arts maneuver, and then in one slow swipe, carved off Mengele's tongue! Blood splattered everywhere, and Mengele screamed so violently, his eyes erupted from his head!

"Now you can't spread your lies in hell about 'following your orders', you filthy piece of shit!" Benny shouted over the gusting winds.

He took Mengele's severed tongue in one hand and his Chalaf in the other and raised both his hands to the sky!

"A gift to those who perished!" Benny proclaimed.

Suddenly a giant bolt of blue lightning came blazing down from the sky and struck Benny's blade!

It illuminated it as the powerful energy of the Lord passed into it and through Benny's body, and then vaporized Mengele's limp tongue right out of his hand!

Amazingly, although he was pounded to the ground, Benny was not injured. He instantly noticed that his smoldering blade had turned from bright silver to a burnished blue tone, and a golden Star of David was now prominently fused upon it! He shrugged off the jolt, and noticed the rock crusher was running smoothly and it was ready to get to work.

"Pull the lever and engage the conveyor belt!" Benny shouted to Boris over the heavy winds.

But Boris just stood there paralyzed.

He just looked back at Benny as the wind gusted and the thunder and lightning raged around them!

"Boris, start the conveyer belt, and let's finish this Nazi scumbag!" Benny shouted.

"I can't... I can't do it!" replied Boris.

"Are you crazy! This son of a bitch killed your sons! Pull the lever!" Benny shouted.

"I thought about how I was going to kill this sinister demon for so many years, but now I realize I am not a murdering beast like him! I can't take his life...as much as he deserves to be slaughtered!" cried Boris.

Boris began to weep and he broke down as he was overwhelmed by emotion.

He had been living his life obsessively hunting down this putrid being, and now that he finally had him in his grasp, he couldn't become what the Germans and their conspirators were, bloodthirsty murderers.

Benny shook his head in disbelief.

"I understand how you're feeling, friend," Benny compassionately stated.

Benny managed to stagger through the high winds over to Boris and he embraced him.

All the pain and anguish that was bottled up inside of Boris was now pouring out.

He buried his face into Benny's chest and cried as Benny held his head against him.

As they were distracted, Mengele was squirming and trying to roll off the conveyor belt, hoping to slip away.

Benny stretched his leg over to the control lever, as he held Boris, and with a tap of his foot, Benny engaged the conveyor belt. It lurched then slowly engaged and began to travel towards the mouth of the rock crusher.

As Mengele suddenly felt the belt moving, he realized that he was heading directly into the iron jaws of the massive machine!

Desperately, he tried to break free of his restraints!

But the belt was steadily moving along, carrying him closer and closer to his brutal demise!

He was only seconds away from being delivered into the massive mouth of the crusher!

Benny then let go of Boris and pulled the lever, halting the conveyor belt, as Boris then regained some of his composure.

Mengele continued awkwardly screaming and spitting out pints of blood, as the wind, lightning and thunder continued releasing their raging fury all around us!

"Dr. Josef Mengele, you are hereby sentenced to death for crimes against humanity! Prepare yourself as you had prepared countless victims to cruel and inhumane torturous deaths! Their blood is on your hands! Now you will die a horrendous death by the hands of the people you murdered, and justice shall be served," shouted Benny.

Benny once again engaged the lever of the conveyor belt, and the belt began slowly moving, carrying Mengele into the mouth of the crusher!

The storm furiously raged on as the enormous iron pistons were beating up and down as Mengele was fed into the gaping mouth of this powerful machine. It effortlessly began smashing Mengele's feet, slowly inching its way up his body and pulverizing his legs.

Yet again Benny stopped the belt, prolonging Mengele's brutal dispatchment to hell. Mengele continued to shriek and carry on like a mad man as he desperately tried to roll off the conveyor belt!

"Dr. Mengele, there is a place deeper than the fiery tar pits of hell awaiting you!" Benny shouted.

And he engaged the conveyor belt for the final time. Mengele's body began inching forward once again, and it continued on its path into the crusher! Boris finally came to his senses and rushed over and took hold of Mengele's sweaty black hair, and with his enraged face he stared deeply into his agonizing eyes! He was remembering the way Mengele had maniacally laughed at him when his henchmen tore his children from his grip, and then once again when he picked up his precious little boys from the pile of dead children in his sadistic laboratory.

"Now you Mengele, are the one in pain and suffering, and now do you hear my fury you son of the beast!!" Boris raged as Mengele was slowly being devoured by the rock crusher!

Inch by inch Mengele's body was pulverized!

Knees, thighs, his groin then hips! His internal organs splattered like water balloons as the conveyor belt slowly inching along into the rock crusher and the rest of his body soon followed.

Hideously, Mengele continued screaming vulgar diabolical profanities as if possessed by a vial demon, all the way to the point that all that was left of him was his decapitated head, and his satanic shrieking only ceased when his vile head finally exploded by the final blow of the hammers.

His mutilated remains passed through the rock crusher as a bloody paste with no means of identifying who or what the sewage once belonged to.

"What are we going to do with him now?" Boris questioned.

"Nothing. Leave him for the flies and maggots," Benny said.

Despite the storm, we heard police sirens in the distance getting louder and coming our way.

"We'd better get out before the police get here!" my father shouted.

We all jumped into the back of the truck. Boris, who was in the driver's seat, was quickly driving the vehicle away.

We could hear that the sirens were getting closer as the Sao Paulo police were on their way!

The winds turned even more violent and picked up more force as they began to develop into a raging tornado! The wind was spinning faster and faster as giant bolts of lightning were branching out from the center of its funnel!

"Hurry! We have to meet Fritz at the airport before the police get here!" my father shouted over the heavy winds.

Boris quickly sped away, recklessly driving over the piles of dead Nazi bodies.

We left the mining compound and we raced towards the airport. While watching out of the back of the truck, we could see the twister growing and spinning faster and faster! It was turning into a gigantic funnel of fire and lightning! The earth began to shake as it bore down onto the tainted soil of the mine, consuming all of the remains of the evil entities that we had left behind there.

Suddenly, the storm became silent, and then a tremendous blue lightning bolt once again reached down from the heavens followed by the loudest thunder bang we had ever heard! It pounded down on the earth, and drove the tornado which had engulfed the sinister remains of the mine down into the burning dumpster of hell!

But then, in an instant, the storm spiraled upward and darted back up into the heavens as quickly as it came.

The mine was completely gone, and the earth was cleansed.

Once we were a safe distance away, we all realized what we had witnessed. The power of the almighty God, and we were the "Chosen" ones.

Chapter 17

My father held Hanna as she started to come out of her hypnotic trance.

She told us she had no recollection of being kidnapped. But she remembered something about a broken down vehicle near our home.

The same went for Benny's children. However, they added that they were being strong like their mother, and Benny made a grimace as he felt offended.

We continued speeding down the bumpy roads of Sao Paulo, until we finally could see the bright lights of the airport.

We entered through an unattended cargo gate, and my father directed Boris to head to the freight area, where Fritz would be waiting for us.

Boris recklessly parked in a dimly lit loading area, and then we all jumped out of the truck and began running toward the cargo hanger where Fritz was waiting for us.

Benny was carrying Shimon's draped body over his shoulder when my father noticed that Boris had remained in the truck.

He was just sitting there motionless behind the steering wheel, watching us run to the airplane hangar.

My father stopped and quickly returned to get him, as we could hear the police sirens approaching.

"What's the matter, landsman?! Why are you sitting here, come on, let's go!" my father shouted.

"Watchmaker, I spent the past ten years grieving and mourning over my wife and children. For all that time, my whole life has been consumed with finding and killing, Mengele.

"Now that it is over, I have nothing else to live for. I want to be with my family now," Boris solemnly stated.

The police sirens were getting louder!

"Come with us, now!! Your family would want you to live! You'll have plenty of time later on to be with them again!" pleaded my father.

Boris reached his hand out to my father. Significantly, this time it was with his right hand.

"Thank you for everything, Watchmaker. But, I just want to go home and be with my wife and children once again," Boris mournfully stated.

My father nodded his head in an understanding manner and shook his right hand firmly.

"Peace be with you friend," shouted my father and he left Boris and ran toward the hangers.

By now the police were almost upon us. Boris engaged the transmission and quickly pulled away, circling the truck toward the entrance of the freight gate.

Fritz was there waiting for us and he started his plane's engines. Several police vehicles and military trucks, armed with machine guns, entered through the gate and began firing at us as we boarded the plane.

Boris fully accelerated the truck and drove straight toward the vehicles.

My father stood watching Boris's final act of heroism as Benny and I closed the plane's heavy door.

As the plane began to pull away, a massive explosion ensued, and lit up the entire area around us!

Fritz raced the throttle of his plane, and we fully accelerated down the runway, and we were airborne in a matter of a few seconds.

The plane began to circle and we could see the burning wreckage of Boris's truck and the police vehicles, as firemen raced toward the scene.

We were saddened that Boris chose to give up his life for us, but hopefully he was reunited with his loved ones, and is in a better place as he had hoped. We sat between boxes of cargo as the plane left Sao Paulo air space and we prayed that we would make it home safely.

My Father, Hanna and I sat together in silence.

We could hear Benny and Sonya quietly speaking Hebrew to their children. My father was staring down at the Red Diamond ring on his finger. Had he not had the inclination to bring it, without it we all might all be dead.

He twisted the ring off his finger and handed it to me.

"Where are we going to buy our gems from now?" he facetiously asked.

I sat there, shrugged my shoulders, and made a silly face as I put the ring in my pocket.

The plane was dimly lit and its engines droned in the background.

There was no celebration or talk about what had taken place.

Just as Benny's father, the Shecket, would slice an animal's throat, it was for a purpose. It had to be done.

The same was true with our mission of killing Heim and Mengele. It had a purpose, and it had to be done.

As Benny sat next to Sonya, she quietly began softly singing a song in Hebrew as they rocked their girls to sleep.

Hanna snuggled up against my father and closed her eyes.

I sat quietly in thought and observed everyone as they rested.

I could hear the ticking of my father's watch and it brought back more memories of our incredible journey.

We had been through so much. We witnessed the many faces of death, and endured the worst kinds of evil.

But why were we chosen to survive while others perished?

Maybe we were just lucky, or maybe God was watching over us and it was his will. I don't know.

But one thing I do know, my father was our pillar of strength. He was the guiding light who led us through this horrific garden of evil.

Even though sometimes I questioned him, he always knew what was best for us. His strength, wisdom and determination enabled us to not only survive, but to fight back.

My father is my hero, even though he is humble about saving our lives. If it wasn't for him, we know we would all be dead by the hands of the Nazis and their collaborators.

Î put my arm around him and kissed him on his cheek. He slowly opened his eyes.

"What was that for?" he whispered.

"I love you, Papa. I'm so proud you are my father and that I am your son. Your guidance and wisdom molded me into the man I am today. I will be forever grateful," I said, and then I began to weep.

He pulled me next to him, put his arm around me, and embraced both Hanna and me tightly.

"Someday when you are a father, you will understand the powerful force of love a father has for his children. You can't understand yet, how a parent could be so devoted...to protect and sacrifice, and drench a child with love. Even to die so that your child could live on. You can't know this type of bond until you are holding your own child. Then you will understand what it is to be a father. Boris was also a perfect example of that kind of love and devotion," he said softly.

I smiled and rested my head on his shoulder.

He makes me feel safe. Then peacefully, I drifted off to sleep.

The following morning, when we finally arrived in New York, several Mossad agents, dressed as ELAL airline personnel were waiting for us.

We all hugged and kissed, and said our goodbyes.

The agents carefully took Shimon's body and escorted Benny and Sonia with their children onto the tarmac, and then onto a transport vehicle that would take them to an awaiting ELAL jet, heading back to Israel.

"Hey Sonia!" I shouted, as they departed.

She smiled and looked back at me.

"Tell your girlfriends, I'm coming to Israel!"

She became very excited and clapped her hands.

"Mazel tov! When?!" she exclaimed.

"I'll see you, after Benny cleans out the bunker!" I replied.

She laughed and waved as they pulled away and drove off.

Fritz wandered down from the steps of his airplane carrying a few bottles of seltzer and he approached us.

"I just wanted to see if you might need these drinks, Jacob. The last time we flew together you and your sister were green as the grass!" chuckled Fritz.

"Please don't remind me, It's been over 10 years and I still hate sardines!" I joked.

"Me too!!" Hanna added.

My father thanked Fritz again, and then he ceremoniously tossed him a large gold coin, as he had done years ago when he had flown us out of Poland.

"You know Watchmaker, you're not so bad for a Jew," Fritz jokingly stated.

"You know something Fritz, you're not so bad for a German, either!" my father warm heartily replied.

And then we all hugged, said our goodbyes, and we left for home.

Chapter 18

The sun was shining down on us as we rode back from the airport in a taxi to our home in Queens.

It was an awkward feeling, where one minute we were violently killing a number of war criminals, and then suddenly we returned to our normal dull life.

We took some time off as we usually did for the rest of the month of August, and reopened our store approximately 4 weeks later, in September, right after Labor day.

It's a busy time considering many of our customers were waiting for us to return from vacation.

The jewelry district was busy as usual, and the streets were crowded with all sorts of people.

I noticed a large homeless man who suddenly appeared and began wandering and panhandling on our block, his name was Frank.

He was dressed in an abused dark green plaid suit and he was wearing an oversized filthy hooded black trench coat over it.

I thought it was odd for him to be wearing such a long coat, since it was the end of summer and still fairly warm, but then again, I've seen these vagrant types often wear all their clothing at once so they don't get lost or stolen. Most of the homeless vagrants in the city live in the shelters and are clean, however this vagrant man lived on the street and was totally disgusting and filthy.

His clothes were covered with grime, liquor stains and vomit.

While his face was barely visible as he hid it behind his mangey long blonde hair, which was completely draped over his face.

He kept his head covered with a black "I Love NY" baseball cap, which he tipped down over his eyes along with an oversized pair of mirrored aviator sunglasses that were broken at the bridge and held together with black tape.

His grimy tarnished face was completely hidden behind a gnarly wild beard, which was filled with all sorts of disgusting food particles, debris and mucus among other things that were collected in it.

And lastly, on his feet he wore a pair of dilapidated black and white wing tipped patent leather shoes, that appeared to be about three or four sizes too big for his sockless feet.

There was a horrible stench that reeked of sour garbage and vomit that lingered over him like a green cloud, and it was clear that he hadn't had a bath in over a century.

Each and every day he could be found roaming up and down our block, panhandling for money. And he made it a practice to constantly stop in front of our store, and he would peer in through our glass door or front windows and watch us.

Sometimes he would tap a coin on the glass, hoping to attract a wealthy customer's attention, who sometimes would give him a hand out when they left the store.

Unfortunately, to make matters even worse for us, Frank was also sleeping in a large cardboard refrigerator box, right in front of our shop. No matter how many times we called the police, they never did a thing about him.

One afternoon my father finally had enough and approached the vagrant and offered the man a proposition.

"Frank, may I have a word with you?" my father asked.

The man grunted back at my father and blankly stared into his face through his mirrored aviator sunglasses and his hairy face.

My father reached into his pocket and took out a one hundred dollar bill and showed it to the man.

"I will give you this one hundred dollar bill if you promise me that you will stop drinking and get yourself cleaned up, and in turn I will get you a job and a decent place to live! How does that sound to you?! Do we have a deal?" questioned my father.

The homeless man eagerly nodded and grunted as my father handed him the bill.

Frank snatched up the 100 dollar bill and walked away, heading towards a nearby deli to presumably to get some food, when he made an abrupt turn, and then proceeded directly into a gated liquor store, and then shortly after he returned to his cardboard box with a one hundred dollar bottle of Courvoisier Cognac!!

My father threw his hands up and gave up!

Chapter 19

It was a Friday afternoon when a beautiful Indian woman in her early twenties cautiously entered the store and waited her turn patiently as we helped other customers.

She seemed nervous and kept looking at her watch.

I was working at the time with a young couple who was interested in purchasing a diamond engagement ring.

The young woman, her name was Lenore, was being impossible.

Every diamond was too small, and she insisted that she had to have a bigger diamond than her sister and the biggest diamond of all her girlfriends!

Her soon to be fiancé, Peter was beginning to sweat profusely considering his budget was well below her champagne taste.

I tried to help the young man by pushing quality over size, but the young woman wouldn't have any part of it.

"My friends are going to talk about my ring behind my back. If it's smaller than theirs, they will say you gave me a speck and you are a cheapskate!

If it looks yellow, they will say you bought me a lemon and you are a cheapskate!.

If it doesn't sparkle, they will say you gave me a piece of glass, and if it's not flawless they will say it's a piece of coal, and you are a cheapskate!!" she complained.

My father wandered over to see what was going on, and he asked if he could be of some assistance.

"Sir, my girlfriend is driving me crazy!

Because of her jealous and materialistic friends, she will only be satisfied with the biggest and best diamond that you have in the store! I don't think I can afford such an extravagant diamond, but it's the only thing that will make her happy.

I feel that the size shouldn't matter as it's a symbol of our love for each other," stated Peter.

Lenore quickly interjected;

"Yes, but it is a symbol of your love for ME, and if you buy ME a tiny diamond, it shows ME you only love ME a tiny bit...on the other hand, an enormous diamond would shout out to the world that you love ME enormously!" she joyfully stated.

"Can I tell you a story that was written thousands of years ago regarding a similar issue?" my father interjected.

Peter desperate for help quickly agreed, while Lenore yawned and had the look of boredom painted on her face.

My father continued;

"A pair of young lovers were sailing in the Red Sea. A sudden violent wind blew and they were both cast out of their vessel! Neither could swim, and so they began drowning in the water. Before they both perished and were consumed by the tumultuous sea, their soul spirits were brought before God for judgment.

The man was a kind laborer who worked hard and earned a modest living as a stone cutter.

He didn't have abundant riches, but he was a righteous and pious young man.

The girl was a cold hearted woman that was materialistic and conceited. Although he knew his love was a selfish woman, he thought he could change her ways over time, and guide her down the path of the kind hearted and righteous.

The woman was completely different from him, she was a selfish gossip, and a fervent coveter who only desired the wealth and riches that her friends, neighbors and what others possessed.

She viewed herself to be above everyone and would stop at nothing to satisfy her gluttony.

She admitted that she was only with her lover because she believed that someday he would build her the biggest castle from his stone work ability, and then afterwards she would cast him aside.

The all mighty placed two large tipping scales, side by side before the couple on a large wooden table made of olive tree branches and exotic tree woods.

Behind the table were three large ornate gates. One made of silver, one made of gold, and the other made of ugly blackened iron.

The silver gate was the gate to life. It was peaceful and surrounded by blooming flowers and fresh fruit.

The golden gate was the pathway to glorious Heaven, and was surrounded by a magnificent rainbow and heavenly creatures. However, the ominous black iron gate was the gateway to Hell! It was morbidly smokey with its blazing fires and smoldering brimstone, and devilish creatures that were crawling on 4 legs within it!

God then ordered the pair to each stand before the table, and for each of them to stand in front of one of the tipping scales.

On the left pan of each of the two tipping scales, God placed a single gruesome human eyeball upon it.

The scales were cinched in the middle, so that the pans could neither move up nor move down until the cinch was released.

Between the two scales was a fantastic golden treasure chest the size of a bushel of pomegranates, and perched on top of the chest were two pure white doves.

God then instructed the couple to lift the chest's lid and view its contents.

The woman wasted no time and harshly brushed the birds off the lid, and the pair flew off in a perfect circle and returned, perching themselves onto one of the small olive branches that was protruding up from the table.

The materialistic woman's eyes widened and bulged out of her head as she raised the lid, and she salivated over the chest's golden bounty!

It was filled with gold coins, solid gold jewelry and other golden objects laden with fine precious gemstones!

"Won't my friends and neighbors now covet me and my riches, and bow down to my greatness as I pass by, if only I was adorned with jewels such as these!" she selfishly thought.

God then instructed the couple that they should each choose items from the treasure chest to place upon the opposing tipping pan of each of their scales. And, if they should tip their scale in their favor, and raise the pan accommodating the measly eyeball, being that their items were heavier than the one eyeball, they could keep the items and return safely to their home.

But if not, they will have to pass through the gateway to Hell and remain there for eternity.

The woman readily agreed, and thought she had outsmarted God.

She quickly reached over and heaved the entire treasure chest up and dropped it onto her scales tipping pan!

The young man was taken aback by her rash decision, since she had not even discussed any options with him.

She took the whole bounty and left nothing for him to place on his scale.

When he asked her if he could choose something from the chest to save his life, she viciously slammed the lid shut!

"No!! You are going to Hell, Stone cutter!" and she maniacally laughed.

The Stone cutter was saddened and contemplated how it was that he was with such a selfish, and greedy woman in the first place.

"I have no desire for the treasures or the vile life you seek," stated the young man, and he reached over and perched the two white doves on his finger and then placed them gently on his scale.

The young woman heinously laughed at her boyfriend's unfortunate circumstance, as he stood there quietly with his hands clasped together and his head bowed down, and they waited for God to release the cinches which restrained the scales.

With a twitch of God's eye brow the cinches on both scales became unfastened and the pan with the eyeball on the woman's scale swiftly plummeted downward and the chest full of gold rose upward!

Her lover's scale had quite the opposite result, and the pan with his two doves plummeted and raised the eyeball!

The young woman became angry and protested to God!

"This is trickery! How can this be?!! It is impossible that my treasure chest had not outbalanced the eyeball, and the two white doves on his scale did!" she protested.

Then God spoke to them;

"For the selfish and narcissistic, the eye can never be satisfied and will always desire more and more! No amount of gold and jewels can ever tip the scales of gluttony to satisfy the eye of greed. Even that entire chest of treasures which you cast upon my scale could never be enough for someone with eyes as big as yours!" God commanded.

The doves on the other hand represent love, peace and good will. The unselfish and righteous virtues that this young man possesses, and he chose that over wealth and riches!" blasted God.

A wild wind quickly arose and the woman screamed in horror as she was instantly sucked through the ominous black iron gate! She desperately clung onto the treasure chest, carrying it away with her as she plummeted down through the smoking fiery embers to Hell!

The righteous young man was guided to enter the silver gate, and was returned to his boat along with the two white doves where he later found a beautiful maiden that happily lived a modest life, and put the needs of the unfortunate before herself. And, she truly loved the Stone cutter for who he was, not for what she could benefit from him.

My father ended his story by ceremoniously wiping his hands across each other in the air, as if he were casting the filth off of them and now they were cleansed.

Peter nodded his head as he understood the moral of the story, yet Lenore yawned and remarked;

"Can we get back to the diamonds now?"

The young man slumped over defeated and dismally asked me how much was the biggest and most expensive diamond I had in the store.

I informed him that we had a flawless 12.77 carat blue diamond ring that will cost him approximately $235,000 that we kept in the vault.

He reluctantly asked me if they could see the diamond, which really excited his girlfriend.

I sent my father to retrieve the diamond ring and when he returned, I placed the enormous diamond ring on her finger.

"Now that's what I'm talking about!!" she exclaimed.

"Honey, is this the ring that will make you happy?" the young man inquired.

"Oh yes baby!, It's so much money, but I'm worth it!" she stated.

"I'll have to sell everything I own, and use all the money I saved up for college, and take on a third job, but I love you so much, I just want you to be happy," Peter fawned.

"This ring will make me extremely happy, and my friends will be so jealous! Wait, do you have anything bigger?!" Lenore half heartedly joked.

The young man beaming, looked over at me and stated;

"I'll take it!"

I was shocked and couldn't believe this young man was going to spring for such an expensive diamond, and furthermore get engaged to this selfish, materialistic witch.

She began hopping up and down, giggling and carrying on about "her" enormous diamond and how happy she was, and how jealous and envious, her friends will be!

And she didn't let us forget about how her poor demoralized sister is going to take it either!

The young man pulled out a check book from his back pocket and explained that he only had enough money for a deposit today, and that he would leave a check and return to pick up the diamond next week, and then pay for the diamond ring in full, with cash!

"That sounds good to me. Just so we're clear though, the diamond stays here until I have the cash next week, right?" I stated.

"That's right," he replied and the young man began writing out the check.

"How much would you like for a deposit?" he inquired.

"Usually we like to get 10% for deposits, so if it's okay with you $20,000 is close enough," I replied.

His girlfriend continued swooning all over him, as my father took the ring back, and she took her final mouth watering gawk at the humongous diamond ring before my father disappeared with it, returning it back to the vault.

The young man quickly wrote out the check, and handed it to me.

His girlfriend was crawling all over him, whispering in his ear and crudely stating what she was going to do with him once they returned home!

As I glanced down at the check, I noticed that instead of writing the store name and amount, he wrote a note;

"Sir, I'm sorry to waste your time, but I learned a valuable lesson today from your wise father.

And he had drawn a picture of the 'Gates of Hell' on the check and the two doves, and one of them was flying away!

He watched me as I looked the check over, and I smiled.

"Oh Miss, I have to say something before you leave!" I stated.

The young man instantly froze when he heard me say that to her.

"Congratulations! I'm going to need to measure your finger so I can have the ring sized and ready for you next week," I smugly stated.

"Oh yeah, the ring size!" Peter laughed, and Lenore cheerfully paraded out her left hand, and allowed me to measure her ring finger.

The young couple danced away as Lenore clung to his arm, and continued gushing all over him.

Then Peter looked over his shoulder and winked at me as they walked out the door.

"What's going on?" my father asked.

"Your story opened his eyes about the girl, she thinks he laid out a hefty deposit for that big diamond ring, but instead he tricked her and gave me a blank check. He wanted to get another few days of "Cajoling" out of her before he ends his relationship with her next week," I stated.

"Do you think he might change his mind and come back for the diamond?" my father asked.

I made a silly face and replied "Maybe?...Not!!"

Chapter 20

The young Indian woman who had been patiently waiting finally approached me and asked me if I could help her.

I initially thought she was going to ask about returning a diamond engagement ring from a broken engagement or an expensive piece of jewelry. That seemed to be the norm for when we return from vacation. That's basically how our day was going.

"Hello Sir, my name is Seema. I am Mr. Kesh's daughter," she softly stated.

I was stunned to see the young woman, and although Kesh would sometimes speak of her, I always thought she was a young teenager not a beautiful young woman.

It was awkward facing the girl since she resembled Kesh very much, and we were responsible for his disappearance.

"Hello Seema, your father speaks of you all the time, how old are you now?" I inquired.

"I am 26, but I am here today seeking your help, Sir.

The beginning of August, my father traveled to South America to buy gemstones, and we have not heard from him since.

I contacted a number of his sources in Brazil, and it seems he was there, but after August 2nd, no one seems to know what happened to him," she stated.

"Hmmm, that's very strange. I'm sorry to hear that. You know there are a lot of bad people in South America.

Did you call the police?" I asked as I professed to be concerned.

"Apparently he wrote down on his calendar that he was going to an Emerald mine in Sao Paulo on August 2nd, but I can't seem to get much information from the authorities, other than there was a massive tornado that destroyed the mine, and I am concerned that maybe my father was killed while he was there," she nervously stated.

My father noticed me speaking to Seema and he approached us.

"Dad, this is Seema...Mr. Kesh's daughter. They lost track of Mr. Kesh and they are worried something terrible has happened to him," I stated.

"Oh no Seema...what can we do to help you?" my father inquired.

"Sir, my mother needs money to pay for our expenses, and without my father we have no source of income.

My mother is asking his jewelers to help us liquidate some of our stock. It will be very lucrative for you and it will help out my mother immensely," she pleaded.

"But of course we will help you," stated my father.

"Oh thank you, Sir. Would it be possible if my mother and I come tomorrow after you close and meet the both of you here?" she inquired.

"Yes, even though it's Saturday and the Sabbath, come at 4 o'clock. That's what time we usually close on Saturdays, and it will prevent us from being disturbed by customers. I don't think God will mind us buying gemstones on the Sabbath to help you out, but I can't guarantee how much we can buy," my father stated.

"Anything will be appreciated and it will help my mother, Sir," she replied and she shook our hands.

"By the way, my father told me of the rare Red Diamond you purchased from him...Is there a chance I might see it? I have never seen one, and he spoke so highly of it's incredible beauty!"

At that moment the doorbell jingled and Hanna, who had just finished her day at school walked into the store carrying her book bag.

"Hanna, come over here, this is Seema, Mr. Kesh's daughter," I announced.

Hanna pretended not to know of her father's demise and cheerfully joined us.

Seema became uncomfortable as Hanna approached her, and she turned away avoiding eye contact as she reached out to shake her hand.

"Hi, I'm Hanna, I've heard so much about you, but unfortunately we have never met."

"Yes, it is unfortunate, but I really have to leave now. My mother is waiting for me to come home and she is all alone.

We can talk more if you join your brother and father tomorrow. They are going to buy some of my father's goods," she stated.

"Oh, are you and your father getting together with my father and brother?" Hanna coyly inquired.

"Mr. Kesh has been missing and they fear he might be dead. We are meeting up with Seema and her mother to buy some gems from them, so they can pay off some of their bills," I sadly replied.

"Oh, no...I'm so sorry, I really loved your father," Hanna sarcastically stated.

"You should come too, my mother would love to meet you and maybe you will see something you will like to buy as well. Come to think of it, I'll bring a special gift especially for you!" stated Seema.

"I will try to come too, sometimes I work here on Saturdays," replied Hanna.

"Very well then. Thank you and see you at 4 o'clock tomorrow afternoon. Please don't forget about the Red Diamond," she stated to my father, and she quickly left the store.

"Dad, there is something really familiar about Kesh's daughter and I know I've seen her before," Hanna stated.

"Maybe you are just imagining it, since these people from India are everywhere now," my father replied.

She shrugged her shoulders and dismissed it.

"Yes, maybe you are right," she hesitantly said.

"That was really awkward! Do you think she knows that we were supposed to meet Kesh in Sao Paulo? He must have discussed it with his wife, don't you think Papa?" I questioned.

"Maybe not, I don't think even Kesh would want his family to know what a snake he was, luring us down there to be killed," my father replied.

"I don't know, but we'll meet with them tomorrow, it would be a good cover up to help them out," I stated.

"I want to be there too, there is something about that girl that is not sitting right with me," stated Hanna.

"She is definitely her father's daughter, did you notice how she pitched Hanna to come and buy some 'things' too!" I chuckled.

"Is it possible they could be even more aggressive sales people than Kesh himself?" my father laughed.

Suddenly all the clocks began to chime and it was 5 o'clock, closing time.

Because it was Friday we try to get home before sunset when the Sabbath begins.

Although Hanna lights the Sabbath candles every Friday night, we really don't honor the Sabbath the way we used to, or the way Benny still does.

When we first opened the store we would always close on Friday, just before sundown, and stay closed through Saturday for the Sabbath day, which ended late Saturday at sundown.

But because Saturdays are a very busy shopping day for most of our customers, and we believed it would become a very lucrative day for us, we broke tradition and now work on Saturdays and take Sundays off instead.

Benny calls us the "Hebrew drop outs," but he is very extreme about observing the Sabbath, and won't even turn on a light switch or answer the phone until the sun is completely down on Saturday, and the Sabbath is over.

Chapter 21

As we drove home, Hanna kept insisting that she had met Seema somewhere before, but still could not put her finger on it or remember from where.

When we pulled into our driveway, I noticed our front door was swinging open and all the lights were left on in the house!

My father and I jumped out of the car, and we raced into the house.

All our belongings were tossed about and it was obvious someone had broken into our home.

"Koby, call the police!" my father ordered.

We searched throughout our house to find what was missing,

but whatever they were looking for, it wasn't televisions or electronics.

Our closets and drawers were ransacked but despite the mess, nothing seemed to be missing.

The police quickly arrived and my father made a comment that at least they show up, unlike the police in the jewelry district.

The officer stated that there had been a rash of burglaries in the neighborhood, and that it was probably just a random act.

"Teenagers looking for drug money," the officer stated.

After a few hours the police finally left, and we had to clean up the mess.

"What do you think they were after, Papa?" I questioned.

"Probably cash and jewelry as the officer said.

Lucky we keep all of that in the store's vault," my father gratefully stated.

"I'd like to call Benny and tell him Kesh's daughter came in today, but I know he won't answer the phone on the Sabbath. I guess it can wait," I said.

Chapter 22

We spent the following day working in the store, despite it being Saturday and the Sabbath. Despite the time difference in Israel, I still could not get in touch with Benny or Sonya.

It was weighing on us most of the day, about what a drag it was going to be to have to deal with Kesh's wife and daughter at closing time today, and them incessantly badgering us to buy their precious goods as Kesh had always done.

It was approximately 3:45. Fifteen minutes prior to our usual Saturday afternoon closing time, when four large middle aged men entered the store, laughing and joking with each other.

They appeared to be tourists wearing New York Yankees baseball caps and carrying several bags of souvenirs from the city.

Just behind them, Seema and her mother arrived, and one of the tourist men held the door open for them, as they wheeled in two large suitcases full of goods.

Her mother was bejeweled with several 22 karat gold bracelets and chains around her neck.

She wore a yellow Sari, the traditional Indian garb, and on her forehead there was a bright red bindi dot painted on her skin.

We had never met Kesh's wife before. He always raved that she was a good woman, although she was not very attractive at all. And I remember him telling us that he was forced into an arranged marriage with her, by their families.

She seemed to have a cold and strict demeanor, and she seemed a bit on edge. But I supposed she might have been upset about selling off Kesh's goods and depressed about his disappearance.

Hanna was too busy to notice Seema and her mother as they entered the store.

She was removing trays of jewelry from the display cases and placing them into our walk-in vault for security.

This was an everyday event, if it happened that someone broke into our jewelry store overnight, the valuables would be protected and locked up in the vault.

In the morning everything was removed from the vault, and again placed back into the display cases.

Our vault was fairly large and it was built in a separate room adjacent to the workshop. It had a massive iron door with a combination lock that would only allow it to open at 9 AM. It was similar to the large vaults you would see in a bank. There were many shelves and drawers which contained our valuables and my father kept his Uzi machine gun, and a host of other weapons which were readily available and at rest in there, loaded and ready to be awakened in case of an emergency.

In fact there were guns hidden throughout the workshop too, but getting to them could be problematic.

My father went over to assist the women and instructed Seema and her mother to bring their suitcases, and follow him back to the workshop, where they could unpack their merchandise.

As they passed an open utility closet on the way to the workshop Seema cringed.

"What's that noxious smell coming from in there?" she asked.

"In the jewelry repair process we use gallons of caustic acids which constantly leak from their containers. I have a supply of large rubberized canvas drawstring sacks which I store the bottles of caustic acid in. It's the rubber coating inside of the sacks you smell, they actually smell worse than the acids!" stated my father.

Seema glanced at the white canvas sacks stacked on a shelf, and the large gallon bottles that were contained in some of them, and they continued on towards the workshop.

I approached the four tourists and notified them that we were just closing, and if there was something quick I could help them with as I was preparing to lock the door.

At the same moment Hanna was exiting the vault when she heard Seema and her mother coming down the hallway and approaching the workshop.

As Seema walked past the vault room doorway, she looked in and noticed Hanna and she quickly turned away from her.

Then Kesh's wife passed by the doorway, and she too glanced into the vault room and saw Hanna coming from the vault.

Instantly Hanna noticed the Red Bindi on Kesh's wife's forehead and everything suddenly became clear to her!

She hastily turned back into the vault, and took hold of her father's Uzi machine gun and ran out, slamming the vault door shut behind her!

Then she charged out into the workshop and immediately planted her feet, placed the butt of the gun firmly against her shoulder and opened fire on the two women!

The gun was jerking back and forth as she lambasted the women with bullets!

My father was shocked and confused, and he dove to the floor as Hanna riddled the two women over and over with more bullets!! Their bodies hideously jerked from the impact, and they quickly fell over dead against the work tables!

"Papa!! These two are the ones that drugged me and delivered me to Heim and Mengele!" she shouted over the raging gun.

When the clip was finally empty, she dropped the gun and ran over to my father.

The workshop now looked like a slaughterhouse, and was filled with smoke, bone fragments and blood splatter everywhere.

"I knew I had seen Seema somewhere before, and when I saw her mother's bindi, my memory was jogged and I remembered everything!

They came to the house just after you left for the airport, pretending that their van was broken down in front of our house. When I let them in to use the phone, they jumped on me and injected me with something!" cried Hanna.

"Are you SURE it was them!!!" shouted my father.

Chapter 23

"**J**a, she is sure, Herr Watchmaker," a deep German voice stated as the four tourists entered the workshop with guns pointed to my head and at my father and sister.

"Papa, I don't think these men want to buy any souvenirs from us today," I nervously stated.

The leader was surveying the room and saw the carnage my sister had amassed.

"Tisk, tisk. Some children never change, once this young girl gets a machine gun in her hands, she is dangerous!" he commented and shook his head in disbelief.

"Watchmaker, allow me to introduce ourselves. We are a group of distinguished commanders of the Gestapo SS.

We have been collaborating with our brothers Albert Heim and Joseph Mengele, and a large group of other German patriots to avenge the deaths of our dear comrades and family members, and for the carnage you caused us during the war.

Your insolence has foiled our recent mission, and we are not happy about that at all. You have been very lucky so far Watchmaker, but now your luck has run out," stated the German.

"If I knew you krauts were coming to visit, I would have thrown a party, and invited my other son Benny and his wife Sonia here to join us," my father sarcastically stated.

"Unfortunately for them, Watchmaker, we have people in Palestine too, they were the ones who kidnapped his children and sent them to Brazil. Now their mission is to kill the Sheckets boy and his entire family as we speak," proudly stated the German.

"I doubt your German flunkies will accomplish that! I believe that his wife alone could decimate your Nazi hairless rodents. And by the way, it's now referred to as Israel," my father jeered.

"Ha ha aha aha aha, we will see about that, Watchmaker!" the German laughed.

His laugh was odd as he laughed like a jackass.

Hanna's eyes opened wide as she flashed back to the time when she was a little girl, and our mother and her were held captive in the barracks at the Willows by the Nazi death squad.

She was forced to sit there with a burlap sack over her head as they raped our mother over and over.

"He was there!! He was there!!" she raged and screamed.

She lunged at the German, but my father grabbed her and held her back!

"Don't shoot! Don't shoot!" my father shouted at the Germans.

"That bastard was one of the filthy pigs that raped Momma in the Willows!! I recognized his donkey laugh!" shouted Hanna.

The Nazi began to bellow his braying once again, as he saw that Hanna had recognized him and it antagonized her.

"I was going to tell you about that a bit later, Watchmaker. But since the "Cat is out of the sack" so to speak. Yes, it was actually me who initiated the idea of utilizing your beautiful wife for the evening," the Nazi declared.

"Maybe if you gave her what she wanted, Watchmaker, she wouldn't have been so eager to offer herself to us," jeered the Nazi.

Hanna was wild with rage but my father urged her to stop or they would kill her on the spot!

She relaxed a bit, breathing heavily from her vehement anger, and they pushed me over to join my father and sister.

"Sit down, Watchmaker. Make yourself comfortable, we are going to be here for a while...well, at least the four of us will be," he sarcastically stated.

We reluctantly sat down on the gray metal rolling arm chairs of the workshop as the Germans cautiously kept their pistols trained on us.

"Who are you scoundrels?" my father questioned.

"My name is Lieutenant General Heinrick Muller, have you heard of me? I'm famous you know," jeered the Nazi.

"Oh yes, I have heard of you Heiny, what an honor to have the Chief of Gestapo scum in my humble store," my father stated.

"Swine! Don't refer to me as Heiny! You shall address me with respect!" Muller snapped and then regained his composure and continued.

"These three men, Freidrich, Zigfried and Der Kapitan, served under me in the Gestapo SS, and they were responsible for implementing the extermination of our many guests in Auschwitz, Sobibor, Treblinka and many more.

Together we were all responsible for killing millions of your people.

Now Watchmaker, today we are here to finish the job my predecessors failed to do, kill you and your children," Muller gravely stated.

He glanced over at one of his henchmen "Der Kapitan," and gave a nod as he looked over at the two suitcases Seema and her mother brought in.

Der Kapitan, was a very large husky gray haired man, with a large box head and a wired bridge in his mouth attached to several gold teeth. He had bright blue eyes, and he wore thick black framed glasses. Across his left cheek was a long stitched scar.

He methodically walked over and placed the women's suitcases on the work table in front of us. Then he unbuckled both suitcases and from one of the cases he began removing all sorts of ropes, wire, and blind folds.

Also in that suitcase was a black leather briefcase with a large red swastika embossed on it, which he also placed on the work table.

The three henchmen quickly took the ropes and tightly bound us to the chairs, as Muller kept his German luger pistol trained on us.

Hanna was petrified and I was afraid she was going to black out, but maybe that might have been a good thing.

"I guess we aren't going to be buying any gems from Seema today," I joked.

"Yes, I was really looking forward to the headache," my father chuckled.

After we were tightly secured, Muller ordered the men to remove the contents of the second suitcase.

There was a small acetylene blow torch and all sorts of large hammers, chisels and monkey wrenches.

"Are you men planning to do some German style watch repairing with your Bavarian watch repair kit, Heiny?

I always knew there had to be a reason why the Germans were so terrible at repairing watches, and now after seeing your tools, I understand why!" my father joked.

"You are a very funny man, Watchmaker," replied Muller.

Unfortunately, you surviving Brazil delayed our plans.

Since you were all supposed to be killed at Albert's mine, we had planned on breaking into your store since you obviously weren't coming back, to retrieve an item that belongs to us.

"Forgive me Heiny, I'm sorry that we derailed your plans.

Had I known of this inconvenience to you, we would have gladly drank those poisonous German beers that Albert had drawn for us!" my father facetiously stated.

Muller then ordered Freidrich to go to the vault.

Freidrich was a hard and cold blooded German. He had a mechanically stiff demeanor, as if he feared nothing and enjoyed killing everything.

They all had a precise maniacal and orderly way about them.

The way they walked, the way they talked, and the way they could easily kill. They were all ruthless and evil demons.

Freidrich walked into the vault room, and we heard him attempt to move the large release lever of the vault as he fumbled with the combination dial on the vault's door.

A few seconds later he returned aggravated, and stated the safe was locked.

"Nice going, Hanna!" I exclaimed.

"When I recognized Kesh's wife, I knew they were up to no good," she smugly replied.

Muller walked over to the work table and opened up the black leather briefcase as it faced us on the table.

Inside the case was an assortment of various torture devices such as a hatchet, shears, pliers, knives and ice picks.

I knew there was a gun in the drawer of my father's watch repair table, which was located right behind us, but we were restrained and it was out of our reach!

"Watchmaker, as you can see I have the means to torture you and your children, but I don't want you to think that we are total barbarians.

I need you to open the safe for me so I can retrieve an item you "obtained" from us.

We can either do it the easy way or the Gestapo way.

If you would kindly open the safe for us, we will simply kill all of you. Although it won't be a painless or dignified death, at least we can eliminate the long and drawn out torture aspect of it," Muller jeered.

"I would certainly like to accommodate you Heiny, but the problem is, I can't open the vault due to the time lock mechanism. The vault can only be opened at 9 AM, and there's no way around it. We'll just have to wait around here till then.

Maybe Freddie can run over to Chinatown, and pick us up some takeout food while we are waiting. Beware though, if you try to break into the vault with your tiny blow torch and German monkey wrenches, I have to warn you that any tampering with the vault could break the fragile liquid phosgene ampoules that are attached to the interior of the vault's door. That poisonous gas would be bad for everyone," my father stated.

My father then nodded to a small rectangular safe next to his work bench. It contained watches that were scheduled to be repaired and some gold watch parts. The door was still open, and attached to the back of the door was a bracket which held several sealed elongated glass tubed ampoules vertically stacked together in a row.

Muller carefully removed two of the ampules and studied them, and he read the words "DANGER!! LETHAL PHOSGENE GAS" that was etched into the glass vials.

He turned to us and jokingly pretended to drop the glass tubes on the floor, and then he "Hee Hawed" once again with his hideous laugh.

The four men then moved away into the vault room, and had a private discussion.

"Papa what are we going to do?!!" Hanna desperately whispered.

"We have to keep working on their minds, they hate being ridiculed and insulted. We have to buy time. Sooner or later they will make a mistake, and we'll have to get at our guns. We'll just have to keep stalling them," my father replied.

"What "item" do you think they are after?" I asked.

"The diamonds from the valise in the airplane, what else?" my father stated.

The men returned, and Muller seemed anxious and frustrated.

He picked up an odd looking pair of pliers with large gripping teeth from his briefcase and studied them.

"I'm not going to screw around with you anymore, Watchmaker. We think you are lying about the time clock, or at least you can override it. Now open the safe! Otherwise I will begin extracting your teeth, one by one!" exclaimed Muller.

"Can you make it the third one from the back on the lower left side, Heiny. That one has been giving me a problem for a while, and I was planning on going to the dentist anyways," my father sarcastically stated.

Muller shook his head in disbelief, and then with the help of Friedrich, who quickly seized my father's head, he began prying his mouth open with his bare hands, as Muller proceeded to insert the pliers into my father's mouth!

Muller then grabbed hold of a rear tooth, and tugged and twisted at it until he finally yanked out one of my father's molars!

My father remained somewhat collected, despite the pain, and then spit out the blood from his mouth onto Muller!

"Muller you idiot! You extracted the wrong tooth, it was the one on the other side!" my father facetiously jeered as he spit out more blood.

"Here Zigfried, make yourself a pendant from the Watchmakers tooth!" Muller laughed and he tossed the tooth to the Nazi.

The four men took another short conference, and they whispered to one another as they occasionally glared back at us.

Things were going very badly for us, and I desperately looked at the clock. It was 5:17, the sun was setting, and so the Sabbath had ended.

"Papa are you alright?! I'm afraid that we are being punished by God for working on the Sabbath!" I said.

"It's not the first time I had a tooth pulled like that, remember Schwartz our hack dentist in Poland! Muller's technique was less painful than Schwartz! And, maybe you're right about the Sabbath. We have been sinning by not observing the Sabbath for some time, and especially for making money," my father said.

"God if you help us get through this situation alive, I promise no more working on the Sabbath for us!" I proclaimed.

"Amen," agreed my father.

The four Nazis returned and gathered around us.

"So how about it, Watchmaker, are you ready to open the vault now?" stated Muller

"Heinrick, if you tell me what you're after, I may be able to accommodate you, since the item you seek may not even be in the vault," replied my father.

"It must be in there, we ransacked your home and it wasn't there," replied Muller.

"So that was you guys?! Thanks for leaving the lights on, now our electric bill is going to be sky rockets this month!" I sarcastically stated.

"Okay, Watchmaker. I'll tell you what we are after...

Kesh requested $50,000 for his services to get you and your family to Brazil.

It was quite a large sum of money even for us, and we didn't have it.

The only thing of great value that I had in my possession was Hitler's Red Diamond ring.

It was a gift to Adolf from Hermann Goring, his good friend and accomplice.

Hermann had most likely pillaged it from your Jews, but oddly the diamond was white when he gave it to him. As time went on, the longer Hitler wore the ring, the diamond began turning red.

Sadly, I was with him in the bunker before he and Ava committed suicide. He handed me the ring and told me to return it to him when we meet once again in hell! I made a deal with Kesh that he could sell you the diamond ring for $50,000 but it would be returned to us after you were dead. Since you didn't die, I am here for the diamond ring, and the rest of your gold and jewels for good measure" stated Muller.

"Gut in Himmel!! I need to sterilize my hand!! I've been wearing Hitler's perverted ring on my finger!" my father gagged.

"God in Heaven, you're right! That money grubbing Kesh! He charged us $72,000 for that diamond! We could have bought it for only $50,000! Boris was right, he did get over on us!" I exclaimed.

"Okay, Watchmaker. So now you know what we are after, now give me the Red Diamond!" demanded Muller.

"Just one more thing Heiny. How does Kesh's wife and daughter fit into this?" my father inquired.

"I told you not to call me Heiny!" Muller snapped again, and then calmed down and continued.

"They were involved with Kesh luring you down to Sao Paulo. His money hungry wife and daughter apprehended your daughter, and we put her into a cargo container moments after you left. They wanted revenge on you for killing Kesh, and they wanted to join us in your slaughter. Now open the vault and give me the ring!" Muller insisted.

"It's not here, it's in the cookie jar on our kitchen countertop," I declared.

"Liar!! Do you expect me to believe you would toss a valuable ring like that into a cookie jar!" Muller exclaimed.

My father glanced at me and I shrugged my shoulders.

Muller returned once again to the open briefcase and savored over its contents, such as a child would savor over candy in a candy store.

He carefully chose a pair of serrated pruning shears.

"Oh good, you're giving up, please be careful cutting off the ropes from us. I don't want either of my children getting scratched!" my father sarcastically stated.

He glared at my father, then he sauntered over to Hanna.

He noticed one of the large rubberized white canvas sacks under the table and picked it up and dropped it over Hanna's head.

She instantly began to panic, as she tossed her head wildly about, desperate to shake it off.

"Ohhhh, now I recognize you with the sack over your head," Muller chuckled, and he bellowed his donkey laugh.

Hanna frantically was able to shake the sack off her head, and her face was bright red and covered with sweat as she gasped for fresh air!

"I would have tied the sacks drawstring cord around your pretty neck, but just as we had done with your mother, we have plans for you later, pretty girl." stated Muller, and he blew a repulsive kiss at her.

He then grabbed her hand, which was bound to the arm of the chair and struggled with her to grab hold of one of her fingers.

He held her hand firmly, and maneuvered her ring finger into the open jaws of the razor sharp pruning shears.

"It will be a shame for your young daughter to start losing fingers over a material object such as a diamond ring!" jeered Muller.

Hanna began to scream wildly and tried pulling her hand away from him, as she struggled with all her might to break free, but the ropes were too tight!

The tension was rising as Muller began braying like a donkey as he eyed my father, and he began aligning the shears on Hanna's ring finger!

Chapter 24

Once again, I began drifting off to another place, as I began to hear the "Ticking sound" droning in my brain, as Muller was aligning the cutoff point of Hanna's slender young finger between the sharp cutting blades of the pruning shears.

The ticking became louder and louder, and it began to echo in my brain as my heart rate began to rise.

My mind raced;

"This time we are not going to get out of this mess, and they are going to torture and butcher us for sure! In a moment my sister's fingers are going to be chopped off by this sadistic maniac!" I painfully thought.

"TICK, TICK, TICK, TICK, TICK…" pounded in my brain!

Muller suddenly stopped and became extremely agitated!

"What the hell is that "Ticking" noise!" he shouted.

I was stunned! How could he hear the "Ticking" sound coming from my brain! I exclaimed to myself.

"It sounds like it's coming from the front of the store!" stated Zigfried.

"Go see what it is and turn it off! It's annoying and gives me a headache!" shouted Muller.

The Nazi raced toward the front of the store, and the "Ticking" sound became louder and louder as he approached the front door.

By this time it was dark and desolate outside. The once busy streets had calmed and the sidewalks were now abandoned as the entire area was closed. Zigfried noticed that Frank the vagrant bum was peering in through the glass door, and rapping a silver coin against it, creating the crisp "Ticking" sound.

Over and over, he continued rapping it on the smooth glass surface of the door!

The Nazi villain approached Frank, and ordered him to stop it and leave! But Frank was relentless, and continued rapping with one hand and rubbing his filthy fingers together with the other, emulating that if he gave him some money, he would leave.

Frustrated with the vagrant, Zigfried reached into his pocket and removed a one dollar bill.

He unlocked the dead bolt on the door, and slightly opened the door a few inches, just enough to pass the dollar bill through, and he handed it to Frank.

Instantly he was overwhelmed by Franks foul stench and he grimaced. Then out of character, Frank grabbed Zigfreid's hand and twisted his arm and pulled him outside!

In a split second by means of some sort of martial arts maneuver and a blade, Zigfreid was face down on the sidewalk and blood was pulsating from a lethal decapitating wound across his throat! Frank knelt with one knee on Zigfreid's back, and whispered something into his ear as he still continued to firmly hold his arm backwardly erect. Just prior to his death, Frank viciously twisted Zigfried's arm, breaking it out of its socket and then snapped his elbow backwards, breaking it in half over his knee for good measure.

He then shoved Zigfried's body into his cardboard box, which was on the sidewalk in front of the store.

Muller seemed satisfied that the ticking had stopped and returned to his malicious endeavor.

He grabbed Hanna's hand once again, and began to again align her finger between the jaws of the razor sharp shears, then….

"TICK, TICK, TICK, TICK, TICK ,TICK…". That aggravating sound began once again!

Muller was infuriated!

"ZIGFRIED, FIND WHAT IS CAUSING THAT INCESSANT NOISE AND STOP IT!!" Muller shouted down the hallway towards the front of the store, and he covered his ears.

There was no response from Zigfried.

"Friedrich, you go see what the problem is, and see if Zigfried had fallen asleep out in the front!" Muller harshly ordered.

Fredrich raced to the front of the store looking for Zigfried and the source of the "Ticking".

"Hey Heiny, you really need to settle down or you might blow a fuse. A big shot like you whimpering like a baby over a "Ticking" sound is not very becoming of an officer of your stature!" I joked.

"Shut up, you idiot!" Muller shouted.

Freidrich entered the front of the store, and noticed a man peering through the front door, rapping a coin against the glass.

"Zigfried, vo bist du?!" shouted Friedrich.

There was no response, but Frank motioned to the man that his friend had left the store and ran away, as he continued rapping the coin. Fredrich carefully approached the door and revealed his German pistol to Frank.

"Go away bum, schnell!!" shouted Freidrich.

Frank refused to budge and rubbed his fingers together once again asking for some money.

Fredrich lost his patience, and finally pushed the door open and pointed the gun into Franks face.

"Now go away you stinking garbage man, or I will put a bullet into your thick dirty skull!" Freidrich shouted.

Fredrich suddenly noticed the massive blood trail on the sidewalk leading into the tattered cardboard refrigerator box, which was positioned next to the door! Zigfried's shoes were inactively sticking out from it, and a small pool of black blood was leaking out and congealing next to the side of the box!

Before Friedrick could pull the trigger on his gun,

Frank instantaneously took hold of it and breached the hammer with his finger, and then twisted his hand in one motion while at the same time pulling him out the door, and with his other hand he drew a blade from over his shoulder!

With supernatural speed he delivered a deadly slash across Fredricks neck, cutting his throat which nearly decapitated him!

Fredrick's eyes were wildly bulging out of his head as he clutched his jaw and throat, desperately trying to reconnect his head to his neck!

In a matter of a few seconds he was dispatched to a horrific violent death as Frank held him from behind and whispered into his ear.

He quickly dragged Fredrich's body and tossed him into the box with Zigfried.

Muller finally seemed satisfied once again that the "Ticking" had subsided and he once again returned to Hanna.

Again he struggled to pick out a finger from Hanna's hand as she resisted Heim, and again he began to align her finger into the jaws of the pruning shears!

"Last chance, Watchmaker, open the safe or she will never play the piano again!" Muller laughed.

"Believe me Heiny, if I could I would! Why don't you pull out another one of my teeth instead!" shouted my father.

Muller was agitated that my father continued to call him Heiny and he began squeezing the handles of the pruning shears!

"TICK, TICK, TICK, TICK,..."

Muller insanely anguished, and paused once again as he couldn't believe his ears!

The nagging "Ticking" sound had returned once again, only now it was even louder than before!

"Friedrich, Zigfried was ist los!?" Muller shouted.

There was no response.

The "Ticking" continued to get louder and Muller was losing his mind and going berserk!

"Kapitain! Go see what is going on in the front, and find out why the men are not responding!" shouted Muller.

Reluctantly, the very large German darted to the front of the store.

It was very dark and the street lights were casting only a bit of light in through the glass windows and front door.

Der Kapitan suddenly noticed a foul stench and a large ghost-like figure arose from behind a showcase! It appeared to be the Angel of death himself, dressed in a black hooded robe and he was rapping an object loudly against a glass display case.

"Who are you?!" questioned the mystified Kapitain as he aimed his gun at the dark figure.

The Angel lifted his arms and shed his hooded robe, revealing his Samurai sword and Hari Kari knife attached to his belt.

"I am the Shecket's boy and the adopted son of the Watchmaker. I am here to execute you as you have slaughtered the innocent victims of the Holocaust," he commanded.

Benny crossed his hand over his waist and retracted his long bright metal Samurai sword from its sheath and it made a crass metallic sound as it slid out from its sheath. With his other hand, he reached over his shoulder and drew his father's Chalaf, which was concealed in its sheath behind his back.

He crossed his blades in front of his face and the glint of polished steel and the Star of David that God had fused onto his Chalaf reflected off of them.

"By my father's blade which was blessed by a blue lightning bolt from God's finger, I hereby pass judgment on you, Herr Kapitan, to a gruesome and horrific death for crimes against humanity. For your part of the sadistic murdering, torturing and cruelty towards innocent men, women and children. I am going to behead you in a moment, and send you back to the smoldering brimstone embers of hell where you crawled out from. Short and Sharp!" proclaimed Benny.

The Kapitain's eyes bulged with terror, when he realized who this supernatural assassin was before him! The big German became weak kneed and terrified with fear! He was well aware of the reputation of the Shecket's boy, and he knew in a matter of seconds his throat would be slashed and his head amputated!

Despite the gun in his hand, he realized that he was doomed to die a gruesome death!

He dismally dropped to his knees, threw off his glasses and began sobbing.

Der Kapitain was despondent by the fact that his vile life was finished, and rather than lose a humiliating battle against the Jew assassin, he knew with certainty it was over for him, and time for him to pay for his crimes.

He cowardly turned his gun to his temple and pulled the trigger, rather than give the Shecket's boy the prize and satisfaction of slashing his throat and decapitating his head!

The loud "Bang!" echoed throughout the store and Muller became even more distressed.

"Who did you shoot Herr Kapitain!!?" Muller hysterically shouted.

But there was only silence.

"Hey Muller, where did everyone go?" I mysteriously joked.

"Shut up you imbecile!" Muller exclaimed.

"Why don't you go out there, and find out why all your men are disappearing," my father chuckled.

Muller was confused and neurotic, and couldn't comprehend where all his men were, and why they were disappearing.

He began to stealthily tiptoe down the hallway towards the front of the store and repeatedly pointed his gun back at us, but then glanced forward towards the showroom floor and pointed his gun there and then back at us!

"Tick, TicK, TiCK, TICK, TICK." The ticking once again commenced, and it was getting louder as it was approaching towards our workshop!

Muller was in a state of dire panic and sweating profusely.

"It sounds like someone is coming for you, Muller," I chuckled, but I couldn't imagine who it was.

He was all alone now, and he kept shouting for his men!

Then the ticking abruptly stopped.

"You should go see who's out there. Heiny, maybe it's the "Dybbuk". The ghost of all the innocent soles you murdered who are now after you!" my father jeered.

Heim pointed his gun up the hallway toward the front of the store. It was pitch black at the other end of the hallway as he moved forward to cautiously investigate the scene.

Hanna quickly rolled her chair to my father and exposed the knot binding her wrist to the arm of the chair.

"Untie me!!" she exclaimed.

My father was able to stretch his fingers from his armchair and loosened one of the knots that bound her.

She frantically began wiggling and loosening the ropes, and finally she was able to free herself from the chair!

"Okay, now untie us!" I exclaimed.

She ignored me as I saw her instantly change from a young teenaged woman into a ferocious warrior!

Her body began to expand and her face filled with rage and fury! Her forehead began to wrinkle, and her eyebrows began to drop as her teeth were clenched tightly!

She methodically grabbed an ice pick and a polished metal hatchet out of Mullers black briefcase of torture. Then she quickly snatched up the rubberized sack which Muller had previously placed over her head, and she tossed in it the Phosgene ampules Muller had left there, and she slung the sack over her shoulder by its cord!

"What are you doing?!" my father exclaimed.

"Retribution!!" she furiously screamed.

Then in a vicious flurry she charged down the hallway after Muller!

He turned and aimed his pistol at her, but Benny shouted "Tick Tick" from the dark end of the hallway, and Muller quickly turned his attention back towards Benny!

Hanna ferociously pounced on his back, as a lioness killing its prey! She wrapped her left arm around his throat as she clenched the ice pick, and she drove it deeply into the upper right side of his chest, and used it to anchor herself onto him as she wrapped her legs around his waist and crossed them locking them together over his stomach.

He pulled his trigger and shot a bullet into the ceiling.

She leaned backward and with the hatchet in her right hand, she began wildly hacking at his shoulder as she held her position on him with the ice pick in her left hand!

He spun and crashed against the walls of the hallway trying to get her off his back, but she was supercharged with adrenaline and she was relentless, as she continued viciously cleaving at his shoulder, until his arm finally ceased to function and was merely dangling there as he finally dropped his gun!

She then changed her grip on the ice pick and pulled it out of his chest as she wrapped her right arm around Muller's throat, and then madly drove the ice pick directly into his left ear canal!

Muller screamed as if he were on fire as he tried to grab at her with his free hand!

"Let me hear the jackass bray now!" she raged.

He screamed an ungodly shriek as she began vigorously bending the ice pick upward and then downward until the handle finally snapped off, leaving its four inch spike embedded in Muller's ear!

Muller desperately tried to remove it, but Hanna raised the hatchet and began chopping at his other shoulder, annihilating the joint, leaving both of his arms inoperable and he was spinning wildly with his blood splattering everywhere!

He finally tripped and fell to the floor, and Hanna quickly removed the canvas sack from her shoulder and wrestled it onto Muller's head.

She made sure it still contained the Phosgene ampules as she tightened its cord tightly around his neck!

"Mephisto!! Help me! I can't breathe! Where are you my liege?!!"

His horrid scream was muffled by the sack as he begged to his pagan demonic god for help!

"Do you still have your plans to use me later, as you did to my mother, you vile ass! Let me hear your 'Hee Haw' now, you filthy beast!" Hanna shouted.

She then aggressively rolled him over onto his back as he was kicking wildly, and she turned her attention toward the lowest part of his abdomen.

She clutched the hatchet handle and then spit on its blade as she vehemently swung it as hard as she could into his groin, over and over again, and she began emasculating him!

Muller screamed in dire agony as she continued to savagely hack and chop at his groin with the hatchet, completely decimating his entire genitalia!

"You won't be needing that where you're going!" she madly shouted.

Benny then crept over out of the darkness and leaned down next to Muller's head as he had done with the other Nazi criminals, and stated;

"Heinrick Muller, This young Jewish girl has passed judgement on you, and you are hereby sentenced to death for crimes against humanity. For the murder and collaboration for murder of millions of innocent men, woman and children. There is a fiery swamp deep in Hell waiting for you, and the rest of your Gestapo vermin! Short and Sharp!" and he nodded to Hanna to finish him.

Hanna spun around and then groped at the sack and felt for the Phosgene ampules.

"This is for my Mother, you piece of shit!!" Hanna roared as she raised the bloody hatchet and turned it backwards, and she began ferociously clubbing it against the sack which was tightly knotted over Muller's head! She continued clubbing his head over and over until she heard one of the glass ampules burst!

"How does it feel to have a sack over your head you wretched Ass! You'll soon burn in hell with the rest of your Nazi sewage!" Hanna raged.

Benny finally approached her and gently lifted her up, and she clung to him and she wept heavily, as he put his arm around her. She was covered in Muller's blood but she was unharmed.

"You smell like shit," she half heartedly joked to Benny.

Suddenly Muller began coughing and convulsing, gagging and vomiting from underneath the sack!

His body began to flop and jerk, and he erratically rolled around on the floor as he was screaming in agony and unable to remove the canvas sack from his head! The gas was caustic and burned his eyes, face and lungs.

This went on for several minutes until he finally shrieked at the top of his lungs, as if a demon was dying inside of his body, and he was released to Hell's inferno.

Chapter 25

My father and I had rolled our chairs near the hallway and bore witness to what was happening!

When it was all over Benny brought Hanna back to us.

"That was you hanging around our store for the past week! Why didn't you tell us?!" I exclaimed.

"I needed to be completely undercover. Had you known it was me, you would have treated me differently. But Papa knew it was me. He said he recognized my nose the first instant he saw me on the street! I made him promise not to say a word to anyone," Benny stated.

"What the hell took you so long, They could have cut off Hanna's finger!! And by the way you owe me one hundred dollars! I tried to buy you some food and instead you wasted it on purpose on expensive Cognac, and you ate from the garbage cans!" my father gruffly stated.

"Papa, I had to wait till Sabbath ended, and if anyone saw you give me the money it would have surely exposed me, and it added to my cover as a drunken vagrant," Benny stated.

I was amazed to the extent Benny went to watch over us, but I'm glad he was there even though he was stinking up the store.

He untied us as Hanna collapsed back into her chair, and she continued crying.

He looked around the workshop, and he noticed Kesh's wife and daughter lying there dead on the floor, and all shot to pieces.

"The apple doesn't fall far from the tree, does it?" Benny stated.

"They were consumed with revenge for Kesh's death and in turn, they were the ones who paid the price. It seems that the Germans and Kesh were in cahoots with the Red Diamond ring. Boris was right, Kesh got over on us." I said.

Benny shrugged his shoulders and began removing his filthy costume, and tossed it out the back door.

"I have to make a phone call," Benny commented and he picked up the phone and dialed an overseas number.

He was speaking Hebrew, and went back and forth with someone and then abruptly hung up.

"They captured the Germans who were stalking us in Israel. As soon as we returned from Brazil we knew there were some loose strings, we had to find those German agents who kidnapped Hanna and my girls, and transported them to Brazil.

The group in Israel was easy to find since the Mossad was after them hours after we landed.

The group in New York was not so easy, so I decided to go under cover and keep an eye on things," Benny stated.

We heard a single knock on the back door, and Benny let a group of Mossad agents into the store.

They had several plastic body bags and quickly placed the dead bodies into the bags and placed them in a van that was parked behind the store.

They confiscated the suitcases and Muller's black briefcase, and reported to Benny that they had already retrieved the two bodies in the box in front of the store.

And in an instant, they were gone!

"What happened to your mouth, Papa?" Benny inquired.

"Do you remember Schwartz the dentist?" sarcastically stated my father.

"Oh, I'm so sorry I was late, next time I'll break my vow with God to save your tooth," Benny facetiously replied.

"Forget it, and we are not Hebrew dropouts anymore, we are closing the store on the Sabbath from now on!" my father stated.

"We made a deal with God," I added.

"So those devils were after the Red Diamond. How did you keep it from them?" Benny inquired.

"When we came home from Brazil, I tossed it in the cookie jar, it was at home on the counter with the bread and tea pot the whole time!" I laughed.

"Lucky those Nazi bastards, didn't go looking for a snack while they were ransacking our house!" my father stated.

"Forget about the diamond ring, If they would have eaten my cookies I would have really gone ballistic on those scumbags!" exclaimed Hanna.

We all looked at her awkwardly as she picked up my father's Uzi machine gun and then she broke down and laughed. Releasing what was left of her pent up emotions.

"Papa, I really believed this time it was over for us. It seemed as though we were seconds away from death and fortunately, God was watching over us, again!" I said.

"And, me!" interjected Benny.

"Papa, PLEASE promise me that this is the end of our crusade, and we are done putting our lives on the line for the sake of revenge and retribution," I pleaded.

My father put his arms around the three of us and hugged us tightly.

"I love you with all my might, but all I can say is…
Maybe??" and he made a silly face.

Chapter 26

We returned to the shop the following morning to clean up and repair the damage that was done to our repair shop. My father began spackling and painting over the bullet ridden and blood splattered walls, while Hanna and I washed and mopped the floors.

From that day on we honored our pledge to God, and committed that going forward we would be closing the store for the Sabbath.

Despite it's high value, we couldn't in good conscience sell the Red Diamond to anyone due to it's evil and sadistic history.

And so the following Sunday afternoon, my Father, Hanna and I took a boat ride to the majestic Statue of Liberty.

It was not our first time there, but it holds a special place embedded in us, freedom, liberty and opportunity.

Although her torch was off limits, we had gotten special permission to go up the ladder that continued up the narrow passage of her arm, to visit the torch's observation platform.

There, from the highest point of her raised torch, we looked out across the broad sea.

We were in awe of the ocean's massive size and beauty. I removed the Red Diamond ring out of my jacket pocket and my father nodded for me to dispose of it.

I spit on it and then threw the ring far into the sea where it would be lost forever.

Oddly, the place in the water where the ring had landed became tumultuous and a small spinning whirlpool and steam began forming around it! The water began to glow and a bright red light emitted outward from within it. Then millions of black slithering eels began to appear from the oceans depths as they were drawn to the tainted ring, and they powerfully thrusted themselves around the Red Diamond and produced a massive whirlpool!

The eels swam vigorously, building up colossal speed until the whirlpool began to expand! It spun wildly with such force and velocity, that it finally began to rise up from the ocean!

The majestic eels continued on swimming with such tremendous speed and force that their color began to change from black to blood red! It was as if the blood of the innocent victims repressed in that red diamond was now being drawn out of it and absorbed into the eels!

The massive water funnel had now risen completely out of the sea, and was spinning with so much force that it began to cast out the red eels!

It spun with magnificent speed, and then rose even higher up into the sky! At the base of the giant funnel, sparkled the diamond ring, however it had been cleansed, and now was brilliantly shimmering white, with no more blood contained within!

Then without notice, the twister violently pounded itself straight down back into the sea, driving down like a screw through the water directly to the bottom of the ocean floor, and then continued drilling down deep into the core of Earth's hell.

We stood there in awe, as once again we remarkably witnessed the power of God before us!

The three of us just stood there silently. Insignificant crumbs compared to the massiveness of the ocean, and the power of God. We stood there high in the grand statue's torch, and held hands as we gazed out across the ocean, and prayed for the blood of those who were trapped in Hitler's Red Diamond ring, that their soles were now at peace and with God.

Chapter 27

Out of respect for Boris, we kept our promise of the secret of Mengele's death.

Only the Mossad knew that we were responsible for destroying Joseph Mengele, Albert Heim, Heinrick Muller and the rest of their evil cohorts.

But the Mossad continued to claim sightings of these demons and doctored photographs of them. Not only to conceal our secret, but to instill fear in the other Nazi war criminals who were still out there in hiding.

They should fear for their worthless lives that they were being hunted, and will pay the ultimate price for their diabolical and sinister actions.

Our pledge to the innocent victims and survivors of the Holocaust. For the men, women and children, who were either murdered or tortured by those sadistic devils from hell. When those putrid Nazi demons are discovered in their tar pits and sewer holes...

The Watchmaker, and his clan of assassins might just show up behind their doorsteps, and viciously pass God's judgment on them for their crimes against humanity, and that justice shall be viciously egregious and painfully gruesome. It shall be carried out by the hands of Benny, the Shecket's boy and his blessed blade. By his wife Sonia. My sister, Hanna. And by me, Jacob.

And especially by our pillar of strength, my father, Joseph...The Watchmaker.

Chapter 28

The following week was ordinarily uneventful.

Our store was busy as we continued on with our business. It wasn't quite the same as I peered out the store's front glass door, watching the busy commotion of pedestrians moving in a hurry in and out of other businesses. Not seeing "Frank" wandering about the block and staking out in front of our store. It's hard to imagine that after such a near death encounter that we have the resilience and fortitude to continue on with our lives, and brush off the death and the violence from just a few days before.

As I stood there by the door daydreaming, I continued watching the hectic ballet of the city. I couldn't help reflecting about all the tragedy and death that trailed behind us. Thanks to God, we have been very lucky.

Hopefully only good things will come to us from now on, and maybe I can find a girl to settle down with. I suppose I'll need to go visit Benny and Sonia in Israel. American girls for what I've seen so far are too materialistic.

I continued watching out the door when suddenly I noticed a long black Limousine roll up, and it parked itself right in front of our store.

"Dad! There's a huge limousine parked right out front of the store! I think it may be a celebrity, maybe Marilyn Monroe looking to buy a big diamond necklace!" I joked.

My father almost fell out of his seat straining to see the car from his work bench, but then gave up and continued working on his watch repair.

It was exciting, waiting to see who was going to exit the limousine. I eagerly watched with great anticipation when the chauffeur exited his driver's seat and meticulously walked around the front of the car, spying for any dirt or debris that may have found their way onto his precious sparkling limousine, which he then immediately wiped off as he made his way to the passenger compartment. He ceremoniously opened the door, and then stood at attention as he waited for the occupants to exit the vehicle. I first noticed the long slender leg of a woman reaching out from the car. Then I saw the top of a large glamorous pink cambric hat, similar to the ones worn by women at the Kentucky Derby, jutting out of the compartment. Then the young woman who was wearing it, eased herself out and turned back toward the open car door. Several other young ladies, all dressed to the hilt in designer clothing, sporting their large Ray Bans, glamorous hair styles and buckets of makeup also exited the Limo. Not to be out done, they were all swaggering their Gucci and Louis Vuitton handbags.

They gathered around the pink hatted young woman and then the entire group began slowly migrating towards our front door.

I strained my eyes, and then I immediately recognized the young lady with the large pink hat!

My heart began to pound and sweat began permeating all over my body at the nightmarish sight of her! It took me back to a place in time when the Nazi's were breaking down the wall in our safe room and a squad of Nazi's were standing there with their machine guns ready to kill us. My heart was sinking and incredibly this could possibly be worse than meeting up with Wolfie, once again!

"Dad!! It's Lenore! She's coming into the store with her materialistic minion!" I shouted back to my father.

"Who's Lenore!" my father replied.

"Do you remember the couple who was here last week shopping for a BIG diamond? Nothing satisfied the girl and she kept complaining that she needed to show off a grand opulent diamond to impress her friends, and then you told the couple the story about the scales of God!" I shouted.

"Oh yes, now I remember her. I thought the boy friend was going to jilt her?" stated my father.

"This is going to get incredibly ugly dad! Get out here, and bring a gun!" I sarcastically stated.

She opened the door and the little bell jingled as Lenore swooped into our store as if she were some sort of celebrity, with her gang of snobby groupies trailing immediately behind her. She annoyingly glanced up at the bell as if it was cheap and insignificant, and she was irritated at the sound it made. Maybe it was too old and ugly, and not as lavish as she would have preferred.

Once they were all congregated in our store, she turned back toward her friends and raised her hands up to the ceiling.

"This is the place! Isn't it impressive!" she gloated.

My father was taking too long and I was really starting to feel the heat! I imagined the only plausible reason Lenore would possibly show up at our store was to pick up her perceived diamond engagement ring!

"Welcome to our store ladies. How can I help you??" I anxiously questioned.

I was so nervous, I swore I could hear that ticking sound reverberating in the back of my skull.

"Don't you recognize me?" she rudely stated.

"Hmmm, I can't say that I do. There are a lot of customers that come in and out of here. Maybe you can refresh my memory," I dumbfoundedly stated.

She became agitated as she heard a few of her girlfriends begin to giggle.

"Are you sure we're in the right place, Lenore?" one of her friends condescending remarked.

Lenore became angry and raised her middle finger at me.

"I was in here last week with my soon to be fiancé, Peter! And he bought that enormous $235,000 diamond ring that's going to be placed on the finger right next to this one! Now do you remember me!" she blasted.

"Oh yes, now I remember you. Uhh, what was your name again?" I sarcastically questioned.

"Lenore!!" she barked.

"These must be all those friends you were telling us about. A very fancy entourage, you have. So where's Peter?" I nervously inquired.

"Oh sure, you remember Peter since he gave you that big fat deposit!" rudely stated Lenore as she rolled her eyes and looked back at her posse of lap dogs.

Lenore reached into her massive Gucci handbag and removed a sealed envelope and handed it to me.

"Peter is going to meet me here shortly, and he told me to give this envelope to you...he said it's part of the surprise," she giggled.

I took the envelope and she proceeded to inform me that her soon to be fiancé requested that they meet at the store so he could propose to her right in front of all of us!

"I had to include my girls since they all wanted to see that humongous rock. It's not every day a girl gets engaged, and I wanted them to share in my joy," she selfishly bragged.

"Okay well, let me go read this letter and I'll be right back," I said.

Some of her girlfriends became anxious and they began whispering into her ear. She paused a moment as she listened and then she spoke.

"Go get the ring so I can try it on before Peter gets here!" she demanded.

"Oh no, that's a bad idea. I think we should wait. It could be very bad luck if you see the diamond before he gets here," I desperately stated.

"But my friends want to see it and I want to try it on, just in case you made it the wrong size! This way when he gets down on his knees and begs me to marry him, the ring will certainly fit and it won't be awkward. Just go get it!" she ordered.

I turned and walked back towards the repair shop where my father was hiding.

"Thanks for nothing, Watchmaker! You left me high and dry with those Park avenue witches!" I harshly whispered.

"I was just letting you have some practice in case I'm not around some day. What's going on?" he inquired.

"Her boyfriend, Peter, told her to meet him here at the store so he could propose to her. Obviously something is going on since we both know he didn't actually put down the deposit to buy her that 12.77 diamond. He gave her a letter to give me, supposedly adding to the surprise," I stated.

"Ohh boy, is she ever going to be surprised! Open the letter and read it to me," ordered my father.

I ripped open the letter and I removed a folded sheet of paper along with two $100 bills.

Dear Jacob,

I'm sorry to drag you into this situation, but I thought that since your father opened my eyes, I had a clever idea. I would like you to prepare a diamond engagement ring which would ultimately cost $200 including tax, out the door and place it into a ring box. In another ring box please place the 12.77 carat diamond ring she thinks she's getting. When I arrive I will ask you to present the two boxes. If she truly loves me she will accept the smaller diamond. If not, close both of the ring boxes and return them to your vault, and our engagement is off and you can keep the 200 dollars.

Sincerely, Peter

"What should we do?" I asked my father.

"Poyer, take the money and go put a ¼ carat engagement ring in a box. Then go get the 12.77 carat diamond ring and put it into a box too," my father jeered.

"Real nice, Dad, calling me a stupid idiot. You can bring the rings out since you are so smart," I replied.

I returned to the group of materialistic gold diggers and informed them that the ring was still in the cleaner and my father would bring it out once it was washed.

Lenore was seemingly disappointed but had no choice but to wait. Just then I heard the bell above the door jingle and Peter walked in.

I was never more relieved seeing someone come through a door, more so than even when Benny lurched out from behind our hideout door and cut Henry's throat!

"PETER! Come on in, these ladies have been expecting you!" I exclaimed.

"What's going on, Lenore? I thought this was supposed to be just you and me? Why is your murder of crows here?" he hastily stated.

"When you marry me, you also marry my friends," she arrogantly replied.

"Does that mean I can sleep with your friends, too?" he quickly shot back.

Oddly three of her girl friends got extremely uncomfortable and drifted behind the group.

"Come on Peter, you know what I mean. They want to be here to share the joy. It's not every day they can watch me possess a huge rock like the one you just bought me!" she replied.

Peter shook his head in disbelief and asked me if the rings that he had discussed with me were ready.

I escorted the group to a glass showcase where they waited.

I then called my father and he approached from the workshop with the two ring boxes, and placed them down on the glass in front of Peter and Lenore.

Lenore was anxious and salivating at the fact that her treasure was before her. But she was puzzled by the second box.

"Why are there two boxes? Are you buying me diamond earrings too?!!" she exclaimed.

"To be honest with you Lenore, I was hoping that after this past week you maybe would have had a change of heart about that enormous diamond. You said you loved me, and it didn't really matter how big the diamond was. I really can't afford that huge rock but if you truly love me it shouldn't matter how big it is. But if your heart is set on that big diamond, it will be over for us," Peter sadly professed.

Lenore demeanor quickly changed.

"Don't ever say that you can't afford something in front of my friends! Got it!!" she harshly whispered.

Then she smiled again and her fake facade once again returned.

He picked up the two boxes from the velvet counter pad, and opened them revealing that in one box sat the enormous 12.77 carat diamond ring and in the other box, the small ¼ carat diamond ring. Keeping both ring boxes in plain view, Peter held the ¼ carat ring in his left hand and the 12.77 carat diamond ring in his right hand, and then proceeded to get down on his knee and presented them to her.

"Lenore will you marry me?" Peter begged.

She gazed down at the two diamonds and was taken aback by how puny the ¼ carat actually appeared next to the 12.77 carat. Her friends swarmed around her to get a better look at the stones and were holding their breath in anticipation. Surely she would not accept anything so miniscule and Peter was going to be kicked to the curb.

She looked down at him and began to cry.

"I know you think I am a heartless selfish, materialistic bitch with no sense of love or compassion! But I do love you for real Peter, and if keeping you means settling for the smaller diamond I accept your proposal.

The gang of women bust out in laughter and began desecrating the diamond.

"It's so dinky! You're going to be a joke when the rest of your family sees what you settled for!" exclaimed one of her friends.

"I don't care, I'm not going to be that woman who goes straight to hell, like the one in the story the Watchmaker told us!" Lenore boldly stated.

"So you were listening. You are making the right choice," said my father.

The gang of women all turned away and quickly dispersed out of the store. Peter cheerfully closed both ring boxes and handed the box containing 12.77 carat ring back to my father.

He profusely thanked us, and I acknowledged that the ring was paid in full. Then they both began marching towards the door.

"Hey wait! Let me put that in a bag for you. You wouldn't want someone to see that ring box and steal it from you!" I firmly stated.

Peter reluctantly handed me the ring box, and I placed it down into one of our fancy bags and handed it back to him.

"Don't you want to try it on to make sure it fits?" I suggested.

"I'm sure it's fine. Thanks again for everything, Jacob. Sorry, we have to go celebrate!" exclaimed Peter, and the couple linked arms and swiftly exited out the door and disappeared into the busy street.

"That was something! You see I told her that story about the scales of greed and it changed her!" my father declared.

"Oh yeah, you think you changed her, do you?" I questioned.

"Well you saw it for yourself, she chose the boy over the big diamond!" my father declared.

"Open the box in your hand, and tell me what you see?" I said.

My father opened the ring box and his eyes just about jumped out of his head! He was holding the ring box with the small ¼ carat ring!

"Goneff's!!! Crooks!! Call the police! They set us up and stole our $235,000 diamond!!" my father shouted.

Relax Dad. About 30 minutes ago you called me a Poyer, an idiot! I raised my hand, and on my pinky finger was the 12.77 carat diamond!

"Genius my boy!! How did you know it was all a scam?! my father exclaimed.

I sensed that the group of women was a distraction for us and they all seemed too phony. Although they stayed together I was constantly watching what they were up to. Lenore's act was way too overboard, and it was impossible that someone even though she was a New Yorker could be that rude and self centered. Then that note from Peter, who was portraying himself as an honest kind soul who only wanted to be with Lenore was hardly believable! When her girlfriend shouted;

"It's so dinky!" and they dispersed and left the store, that was the distraction that Peter was waiting for, and that's when he closed the boxes and switched the rings! When I offered to place the ring in a bag, I saw that Peter was hesitant and so when I reached down to the bottom of the bag, I removed the ring from the box.

They are going to be in for a big surprise when they open that box!

"Do you think he'll come back looking for the $200?" inquired my father.

"No way, why would he? They are both a couple of crooks! The police will be after them. We should call just so they are on the lookout for them."

"I agree! You did good, my son," my father complimented.

The little bell jingled as the door swung open, and Hanna strolled into the store.

"What's going on? You both look like you just found a Golden Egg," she stated.

"It's a long story, let me put this diamond back in the vault. Koby, your genius brother will tell you all about it," my father stated.

Chapter 29

A few hours had passed and my Father, Hanna and I were preparing to close the shop when the door swung open and the doorbell jingled. A short, chubby middle aged man wearing a sad face entered the store and approached us. He was wearing black pants, a long sleeved white shirt and black yarmulke, pinned to his scalp. As he approached the counter I could see that this man was in pain and had an underlying problem.

"Are you the Watchmaker?" The man questioned my father with a very heavy Yiddish accent.

"Why yes, I am," hesitantly replied my father.

The man raised his left hand as if to shake hands the Boris Wilensky awkward way, but then switched and offered his right hand and shook my father's hand.

"I've got a horrible story to tell you," he stated.

"Oh no, here we go again, after all that we had just gone through! I thought we were finally done chasing after Nazi fugitives. And now, here comes a survivor with another horrific Holocaust story. Probably with the knowledge of a sadistic Nazi's whereabouts, and a scheme to kill the heartless bastard that murdered his loved ones! I know that my father certainly won't refuse!" I anxiously thought.

Before I could intervene to tell him that we are taking a break from Nazi hunting, my father interjected and asked the gentleman to tell us his story.

The man began pulling his left sleeve back in order to reveal something. Obviously another Auschwitz survivor who wanted to show us his numbered tattoo on his forearm. I held my breath in anticipation for his horrible story.

"Go on friend tell us what happened, it will feel good to get it off your chest" my father softly asked.

The man paused, took a deep breath and then began telling his story.

"Well, gentlemen and young lady, here's my incredibly depressing story. I came from the village where I once had a grocery shop. Every morning at 6 a.m. I would arrive at my shop and work all day until 5p.m. stocking and selling groceries. Like clockwork each and every day! Never a minute late or early! My life was governed by time.

All day long I would check my wrist watch and proceed with my duties until one horrible afternoon there was an invasion, and my world came crashing down around me! Those German Nazi bastards were coming, and they were going to take everything from me! I saw the handwriting on the wall and decided I had to do something about it, so I fought them!" the man stated.

"It must have been tragic! We know how difficult it was to fight those bastards. Please continue with your story, Sir?" I said, and I braced myself, as I expected the story to become more horrific.

The man continued;

"It was tragic! Those sons of a bitches, I lost everything! My wife, my children! Everything gone!" the man exclaimed.

Then suddenly the man began rolling up his sleeve as if he was going to reveal his numbered tattoo, and that's when I noticed his antiquated wrist watch which was now exposed. As he continued rolling up his sleeve, we noticed that there was no number tattooed on his forearm.

In fact there was nothing there at all. He must have been imprisoned in some other heinous concentration camp, we thought.

"Friend, so how did you survive the Holocaust?" my father inquired.

"Holocaust? What are you talking about? I was living in Greenwich Village over my grocery shop for the past twenty five years. My whole family moved to America back in the late 1920's. I wasn't there when it all was happening," the man stated.

My Father, Hanna and I were both dumbfounded, as we looked at each other and were bewildered.

My father shrugged his shoulders and asked;

"So what is your tragic story, my father exclaimed.

"The man sighed and sadly stared at his wristwatch. When I found out that they were opening up a German supermarket right next door to me, I knew it was going to be trouble for my business! For years I charged whatever I felt like for my groceries and now I was going to have stiff competition right next door to me! So I went to the town hall and tried to fight them!" the man exclaimed.

"But you said you lost your wife, children, and everything?!" I questioned.

"Yes, my business profits were cut in half! First, I lost my store. Then my wife left me for a wealthy hotel owner from out in the Catskills and she took my children with her! I lost everything because of those Nazi bastards! And this is all I have left!" he cried.

He carefully took his wristwatch off and handed it to my father. My watch is not running accurately, I think it needs cleaning. How much will that cost me?" the man questioned.

"That's your tragic story! Your watch is not keeping time?!" my father exclaimed.

"Yes, my watch is going crazy! It's a problem! I had to degrade myself and take a job at that Nazi grocery store, and those bastards expect me to be on time for work every day!" the man fired back.

My father shook his head in disbelief and took the watch.

He quickly looked it over and wound the crown.

"10 dollars for a cleaning," my father stated.

The man's face became shocked and enraged, and he snatched the watch back from my father's hand!

"Gonneff!! I only paid five dollars for this watch!" he shouted and he charged out of the store, knocking the bell off as he left. The three of us just stood there in amazement and then we burst out laughing!

"This is such a crazy business, you never know just who is going to walk into our store!" I exclaimed.

Chapter 30

It was closing time and Hanna stated that she needed to go to the library for some books about American history and asked if we could stop on the way home. My father urged us to go to the library now, and he would close up the shop and catch up on some of his watch repairs that were scheduled to be ready for the following morning. And afterwards, when we returned we could all go out for supper in Chinatown, his favorite place to eat in the city.

At first I didn't feel comfortable leaving him there alone, but he assured me that he would lock the door behind us when we left, and so we put the remaining trays of jewelry in the vault and Hanna and I left for the library.

A short time later, as my father was disassembling a broken watch, there was a familiar knock at the front door. He got up from his work bench and went to the front of the store to see who it was, and he was pleasantly surprised. It was Eli, a very close friend of our family and our wholesaler of fine gold jewelry. He traveled with his suitcase filled with valuable gold items such as gold chains and earrings. Eli was an incredibly extraordinary individual. He was an Israeli war hero who was also a friend of Benny and Sonia. Together they fought courageous battles during the liberation of Israel, and Eli was also a highly decorated soldier who many times was honored for his heroic acts of bravery. He had a heavy Israeli accent and his English was sometimes difficult to understand, but when he entered a room his vitality was immediately evident. He was full of life and appreciated the fact that life was fragile and you had to live it to the fullest each and every day. When he laughed it was a loud boisterous laugh and you knew he was genuinely happy. On occasion he would laugh so hard that tears would run down his face. But Eli also had a serious side, and at any given moment, if a hostel situation presented itself, he was instantly transformed into an ice cold mechanical warrior.

However, if you were fortunate enough to be his friend and have him in your life, you never had to worry, for you were in his hands now and in his family. He had moved to America a few years ago with his wonderful wife and 4 small children, because he felt it would be safer for his family living here, rather than in Israel where at times there was too much terrorism.

My father was excited to see him and he quickly unlocked the door to let him in.

"Shalom, Pa! I saw your workshop lights were on in the back and I knew you must be back there working," Eli stated.

"Eli, come in!! I have so much to tell you about our trip to South America, and the Nazi scoundrels that took us hostage just a week ago!" Joseph exclaimed. And they embraced each other as they momentarily remained by the entryway of the store and chatted.

"Very well, Pa. I have all night to listen to your crazy story! However, I already heard all about it from Benyamin," he jokingly replied.

"You'll like my version better! It will be more embellished," Joseph chuckled.

"Where is Jacob?! I have a beautiful Israeli girl for him, and she has a gun and knows how to use it!" Eli outrageously laughed, as he was aware of Jacobs' joking apprehension of Israeli women.

"He took Hanna to the library, and when they come back you are coming with us to Chinatown for supper. Leave your suitcase here in the vault." Joseph stated.

"How is it that such a righteous and pious Jew such as yourself, doesn't keep kosher and you eat that Chinese chazeri? You know I only eat kosher food!" Eli exclaimed.

"We don't eat the pork, but just about everything else, though. Benny calls us the 'Hebrew drop outs', but let me tell you something, the Chinese really know how to cook! Trust me, God will forgive you, and you're coming with us!" Joseph insisted.

Eli agreed and then continued in, rolling his suitcase full of gold jewelry into the store. However, my father failed to relock the front door, and a young couple immediately barged into the store right behind Eli and knocked the bell off the door.

"I'm sorry the store is closed," Joseph stated, not really paying attention to the couple. However they continued on with their heads hung low and disregarded my father's words.

Eli turned towards them to repeat that the store was closed, and that's when he noticed that they both were holding semi-automatic pistols and aiming them at them!

Instantly Joseph recognized the pair! It was Peter and Lenore!

"Hands up, Watchmaker!" Peter ordered.

Joseph couldn't believe it. After all that we had been through! Our plight in Poland and then South America, and just last week the Nazi fiends, and now a robbery is taking place!

"Take it easy, don't shoot! Take whatever you want! The vault is wide open!" Joseph stated.

"Where is your son, Jacob? That was a dirty trick he played on me, and I don't appreciate being outsmarted! I spent a lot of money on that limo and those Broadway whores for hire!" Peter barked.

"Let's hurry up and kill them, and grab the goods before someone shows up!" exclaimed Lenore.

"Please, please! Just don't shoot us! I am a husband and a father of 4 little children! And my friend is a Holocaust survivor with children as well!" Eli pleaded.

"Just take what you want, and leave. No need to have a murder warrant on you and your girlfriend," Joseph implored.

Peter began to laugh and he replied;

"She's my sister! Do you think I would actually choose to date an ugly bitch like her?!"

Lenore made a sour face and turned to her brother and told him to "Shut up!" And at that very moment all the clocks in the store began to chime at once, which startled the robbers!

Eli saw the opportunity and courageously moved on Lenore in an attempt to subdue them both! Then with no hesitation, Lenore pulled the trigger on her gun and shot Eli directly in the chest! The loud "Bang!" echoed throughout the store!

"Unfortunately for you, ass holes. We don't leave witnesses!" smugly stated Peter as the clocks continued their racket.

Eli was dazed and confused as he gazed down at his wound. Blood began pouring out of his chest and was soaking his shirt bright red! This wasn't supposed to be the unconscionable way he was supposed to die. He was an esteemed war hero. A man of courage and honor. A humble man who hunted down Nazi war criminals and brought them to justice. Shot by a nobody who was a nothing at all! It would have been more dignified taking a bullet on the battlefield from an adversary, and die for a cause. But no, not this way! No this was not how it was supposed to end for a courageous war hero like himself. His life was taken from him by a mere coward, a loser and a piece of human trash. Didn't they know that he was a man of high esteem, a loyal friend and a man who was loved by everyone?! A righteous servant to God!

Eli blankly stared at Lenore who began sadistically laughing at him as his knees began to buckle and his body started to waver. But before his body gave in and collapsed, and before he would lose consciousness, he courageously fought his own body's surge to die! He refused to succumb to death, and somehow he generated spiritual strength! He knew that he had to protect his beloved friend from these despicable lowlifes. These two scumbags had to be dispatched, for they were cruel and wicked vermin.

And so he concentrated and drew deeply upon himself, and became instantly energized and instinctively reacted! He quickly reached out and abruptly wrapped his hand over Lenore's gun and twisted it, pointing it at Peter's head and with his other hand he pulled her finger back and fired a bullet point blank into Peter's skull! Peter's gun went off, and Eli then twisted Lenore's hand back and jammed the gun into her screaming mouth, angled the barrel upwards and pulled back her trigger finger twice! The back of her head exploded as her brains and bone fragments splattered everywhere, and both pieces of human waste had been instantly executed. Eli collapsed onto the floor and then gravely looked over to Joseph and saw that he was lying in a bad way. Barely conscious and motionless on the floor in a pool of blood, and clinging to the fallen bell! He instantly realized that he had been hit by Peter's bullet in the neck. Eli managed to muster up what little strength he had left to crawl over to Joseph, and he fell upon him. They held each other and prayed together. And then a sudden peaceful darkness fell over on them both, and they began drifting off to a wonderful place. A world which was full of love and compassion. A world full of peace and harmony.

Mighty winged Angels were waiting there to greet them, and to embrace them with their comforting wings and open arms. The Angels bowed down to them, and blessed them before they passed through heaven's gate, for they knew them, and that they were noble, courageous and illustrious men. Men of honor and righteousness. And then Joseph and Eli, through wisping clouds and a bright divine light could see their beloved. Their long lost loved ones were waiting there to greet them from beyond the sacred gate. Joseph's Mother and Father with his wife Sarah were there, and were joyfully reaching out to him!

Eli's parents, and his older brother Uri, who were all killed in the gas chambers at Treblinka, were also there. Uri had sacrificed his own life to save his younger brother's life, when he changed places with him and pushed Eli to the right while he took his place to the left, knowing it was certain death for him and his parents. They were also there to euphorically welcome him, too! The force drawing these two friends over the miraculous gates threshold was powerful. They felt love, peacefulness and jubilation. Once again to be gloriously reunited with their loved ones!

And so by the grace of God, these men were comforted. And then he stepped over the heavenly gates threshold, and a bright light shone down upon him and he became an Angel in Heaven. And he embraced and he was embraced by all who he loved and all who loved him.

Short and Sharp...

Novels by B.L. Blocher:

The Watchmaker
The Silver Orchid
Razzle Dazzle